Praise for
The Memory Keeper

"Readers will be drawn to this poignant story that features a heartwarming relationship between a young girl and her beloved grandmother."
— *School Library Journal*

"Characters (especially family and two of Lulu's friends) are well developed, and the plot unfolds smoothly as Lulu gradually exposes Gram's hidden past. . . . Throughout, Camiccia stresses that the best way to hold on to loved ones is by telling their stories." —*Booklist*

"The author does an awesome job of introducing neuroscience in this intricate tale of a family that works much like a cerebral cortex: when one part struggles to deal, another steps in." —*BCCB*

The Memory Keeper

Jennifer Camiccia

Aladdin

New York London Toronto Sydney New Delhi

ALADDIN

An imprint of Simon & Schuster Children's Publishing Division
1230 Avenue of the Americas, New York, New York 10020
First Aladdin paperback edition October 2020
Text copyright © 2019 by Jennifer Camiccia
Cover illustration copyright © 2019 by Aveline Stokart
Interior illustrations by Jenna Stempel-Lobell copyright © 2019 by Simon & Schuster, Inc.
Also available in an Aladdin hardcover edition.
All rights reserved, including the right of reproduction in whole or in part in any form.
ALADDIN and related logo are registered trademarks of Simon & Schuster, Inc.
For information about special discounts for bulk purchases, please contact
Simon & Schuster Special Sales at 1-866-506-1949 or business@simonandschuster.com.
The Simon & Schuster Speakers Bureau can bring authors to your live event.
For more information or to book an event contact the Simon & Schuster Speakers Bureau
at 1-866-248-3049 or visit our website at www.simonspeakers.com.
Cover designed by Heather Palisi
Interior designed by Mike Rosamilia
The illustrations for this book were rendered digitally.
The text of this book was set in Adobe Caslon Pro.
Manufactured in the United States of America 1121 OFF
4 6 8 10 9 7 5 3
The Library of Congress has cataloged the hardcover edition as follows:
Names: Camiccia, Jennifer, author.
Title: The memory keeper / by Jennifer Camiccia.
Description: First Aladdin hardcover edition. | New York : Aladdin, 2019. |
Summary: Twelve-year-old Lulu Rose Carter's memory improves
greatly just as her beloved Gram becomes very forgetful, and Lulu begins
to explore Gram's past in an effort to save her.
Identifiers: LCCN 2018043943 (print) | LCCN 2018050580 (eBook) |
ISBN 9781534439573 (eBook) | ISBN 9781534439559 (hc)
Subjects: | CYAC: Memory—Fiction. | Grandmothers—Fiction. |
Secrets—Fiction. | Family life—Fiction. | Alzheimer's disease—Fiction.
Classification: LCC PZ7.C328 (eBook) | LCC PZ7.C328 Mem 2019 (print) |
DDC [Fic]—dc23
LC record available at https://lccn.loc.gov/2018043943
ISBN 9781534439566 (pbk)

To my mom,
for always seeing me

the human brain

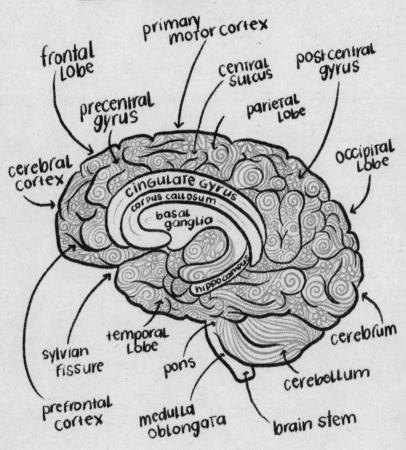

primary
motor cortex

frontal
lobe

central
sulcus

postcentral
gyrus

precentral
gyrus

parietal
lobe

cerebral
cortex

occipital
lobe

CINGULATE GYRUS

corpus callosum

basal
ganglia

hippocampus

sylvian
fissure

temporal
lobe

pons

cerebrum

cerebellum

prefrontal
cortex

medulla
oblongata

brain stem

Contents

The Memory Keeper

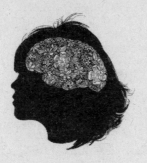

1.
Highly Superior Autobiographical Memory (HSAM for Short)

Turning thirteen and becoming an official teenager in two months is weird enough without having my brain go haywire. But I, Lulu Rose Carter, have a memory that won't shut up.

There are some people who remember everything—or almost everything—about their pasts. It's called highly superior autobiographical memory, or HSAM. It's really rare, like fewer than a hundred people in the world have it. It's not the same as eidetic or photographic memory. A person with

HSAM has memories specific to their past. They might forget little things like where they put their phone five minutes ago, but they can remember nearly every day of their past in vibrant detail.

Not everyone develops HSAM the same way. Some develop it slowly with age. Others might have part of it and then all of a sudden—BAM—the full power of it flips on. Anything can act as the trigger— maybe a stressful event, or maybe something happy like falling in love for the first time. It might even be something like getting lost in a mall parking lot.

Only one person in the whole world knows the secret of my memory. I'm just not sure how much longer she'll remember it. And if she forgets my secret—if she forgets who I am—then who else will know the real me?

My world implodes the week school lets out for the summer. It figures it would happen at the mall. My best friend, Olivia, says anything significant in life usually starts at the mall. She probably didn't mean the parking lot, though.

Gram, Clay, and I have wandered around for the past hour ___ ___ heat turns the mall lot into a waste___ ___ng asphalt. Sticky globs of tar stretch ___ ___th each step, and they cling to the ___ ___ ___oes like a giant web. It's what I ge___ ___ ___hile Gram parked. I wasn't paying a___ ___ ___ow we're lost.

___ ___e the baby's hand." Gram thrusts Clay's ___e.

___ ___aby," Clay shouts.

___ ___ore it was here," Gram repeats for the thou-___ ___ time. Her hands push against her eyes like if ___ presses hard enough, she'll remember. "I parked right here. I know I did."

The sweat on Clay's palms makes them as slippery as butter. I tighten my grip and squint at the sea of cars. We may as well be on a different planet.

I pat Gram's arm softly. "Gram, I think we should go back inside and get something to drink. Clay doesn't look so good."

She glances down at him, but her eyes aren't focused. They're filled with the same fear my horse,

Remy, has when he sees a snake—before he takes the bit in his mouth and bolts.

Clay's whimpers soar to wails, his face a kaleidoscope of red and purple. With all his hollering there should be tears, but his cheeks are as dry as the asphalt. The heat has sucked the tears straight out of his body, right along with Gram's memory.

"I know it's here." Gram turns in a circle; her shopping bags hit my shoulder and tip me into the roasting metal of a car. Clay's hand slips from mine, and he tumbles to the ground.

Before I can pick him back up, a blue truck slows down and idles next to us. The tinted window rolls down, and Mr. Rodriguez, the manager of the riding stables, smiles at us, his mustache dancing as he talks. "Hey there, you need help?"

"Mr. Rodriguez." I smile and try to look normal. *Please don't let Max be with him. Please don't let Max—*

"Hey, Lulu." Max leans across his dad and smirks at me. "You're looking hot. Get it? Because it's ninety degrees and—" Max's dad pushes him back in his seat.

Max's smirk is an exact replica of the one he wore

when we first met three years ago, on the Saturday of my first horseback-riding lesson. He'd worn a Giants T-shirt with a matching hat and made riding look so easy. It was like he could read the horse's mind and make it do anything he wanted. I, on the other hand, could barely stay in the saddle.

Since then he's teased me without mercy. No matter how well I ride now, every time I see his smug face, I'm reminded of the embarrassment of that first day.

"Is he hurt?" Mr. Rodriguez points to Clay, rolling around on the ground and sobbing.

"We can't find our van." The words sound ridiculous as soon as I say them, and if it weren't so hot outside, my red cheeks might be a dead giveaway.

Mr. Rodriguez waves us over. "Hop in, and we'll help you find it. The truck has air-conditioning."

Gram shakes her head, her jaw thrust out with a stubbornness that mirrors my baby brother's. I pick Clay up and stagger to the truck. At almost three, he's getting too big for me to carry, but sometimes it's faster to lug him around than expect him to listen. As soon as I open the door, cold air wraps me in a hug. Clay slumps over and presses his flushed cheeks to the cool leather.

"Stay here," I say needlessly. He isn't going any-where.

Max hops out to help. He smiles at Gram. "Hi, Mrs. Carter. It's Max from the stables. Let me help you inside."

"Come on, Gram," I say. "It's okay."

She blinks at me, confusion blanketing her. I want to shake her. I want to make her snap out of this fog she's in. She's been forgetful before, but not for this long. Not like this.

This isn't the Gram I know. The one who takes charge and bosses everyone around. The one who moved in after Mom had Clay and made me feel loved again. But her blank expression is the same one I've seen more and more lately. And it scares me.

Max murmurs something to Gram as he gently helps her into the car, and it reminds me of his kindness to the horses at the stables. I guess it's just me he teases.

Mr. Rodriguez shifts the truck into gear and flicks a concerned glance at Gram. "Do you remember anything about where you parked?"

Gram's lower lip trembles, and I know I have to do something. I can't let her cry in front of Max and his dad. Gram never cries.

I squeeze my eyes shut and picture driving here earlier this morning. I've always had an outrageously good memory, but I've learned to keep it to myself. When I was really young, I thought it was something everyone had. I found out the hard way that people think it's weird when you remember what they wore six Thursdays ago or what they ate for lunch a year ago from Monday.

Gram is the only one I trust. The only one who really knows about my memory. And she needs me now. She needs me to remember where the stupid van is.

I've become so used to ignoring my memory that it feels strange to work to remember something instead of pushing it away. Even when I don't use it, I always sense it's there. Somewhere in my brain. Waiting.

In the past, some memories would filter through: dates, names, what people did or said. Usually, it was because the day was an emotional one for me. Sad, angry, happy—it didn't seem to matter what emotion as long as I felt it deeply.

But it isn't until right now that I make myself remember every second of *this* day. I've never tried to recall something that happened only a few hours ago. I concentrate, forcing myself to open up the part of me I've kept tightly shut. Scenes of today appear like a movie in my mind. Each scene is separate; each hour has its own place. I experiment, moving the scenes around as if I were watching them on TV. I rewind one and I can see every minute, every second. I don't stop until I find the moment I'm looking for.

My brain skids to a full standstill, and something cracks wide open. I can almost hear the sound of glass shattering. A part of my brain that's been blurry is now completely in focus. Like when Remy breaks into a gallop and the wind hits my face, sweeping away the clutter from my brain.

The Memory Keeper

Click. When I open my eyes, a 3-D map floats in front of me. It's the exact route we took here, right down to the parking spot on the other side of the mall. I blink, but it stays put. I almost ask Max if he sees it too, but then he smirks at me and I know he doesn't. It's as if my vision is divided into a split screen, with one side playing the memory of our van parking three hours ago and the other side showing what's happening this very second here in Mr. Rodriguez's truck.

I know the memory is not really in front of me, but it may as well be. I can see every street, every sign, every car we passed before Gram finally parked earlier this morning.

This is different from anything I've experienced. It's one thing to close my eyes and remember a date or what someone wore, but this is *every single thing*. It's like I have a remote control that changes the channel of my memories. *Click.* Driving to the mall and every turn. *Click.* Every brick, every tree, every store. *Click.* Exactly where we parked, down to the pole two spots to the right of our car. Vivid pictures snap into place; memories line up to wait their turn.

I read somewhere that our brains are like computers. After trying to ignore my memory for so long, did the act of forcing it to work give mine an upgrade? Supersonic Memory Plus, downloaded and complete. Everything is crystal clear, like I'm seeing it all for the first time. And I don't just remember the details. I also remember the feelings that went along with each memory, right down to how I felt when we parked—my excitement at shopping for new boots, my impatience with Clay's whining, my happiness that Gram seemed to be her old self mixed with my worry about her growing forgetfulness. The accompanying sensations wash over me, the blast of heat hitting us as we got out of the car, the smell of popcorn from the movie theater next door, the faint whiffs of cinnamon buns, and the chill of the air-conditioning when we first walked in. It's as vivid as if it were happening to me now.

Or am I imagining it all? There's no way I can

really remember everything this clearly. Maybe the heat is making me see things that aren't really there. That's what I want to believe. Anything else is too much to think about right now. But no matter what it is, I need to get out of this truck with Mr. Rodriguez's overly concerned expression and Max's know-it-all smile. My hand clamps down on the door handle, and I imagine—just for a second—opening the door and jumping.

"Our car is near the Cheesecake Factory entrance," I say, trying not to sound too desperate. "Third row to the right and five spots down."

Max glances over at me, and I bet he wonders why I didn't remember sooner. Why I let my baby brother and Gram wander around aimlessly in the baking heat. Clay slouches on me, his warm cheek pressed against my arm. His breaths come out in soft, shuddering sighs that signal he's asleep.

Every nerve of my body quivers as if my skin were too weak to keep all my feelings inside. I blink away a prickle of tears. I can't cry. Max will think I'm as much of a baby as Clay is.

I dig my fingernails into the palms of my hands. Olivia says the trick to not crying is to distract yourself. She usually does this by online shopping with her mother's credit card. Olivia is the happiest person I know, always smiling and joking, so there must be some truth to it.

We find our van exactly where I said it would be. The floating map folds behind another memory of how to get home. I want to examine it, poke at it, see how far the map goes. I've tried so hard to ignore my memory in the past, but pushing away the need to replay a random day that happened a year ago, two years ago, five months ago is nothing compared to this. I rub my forehead and wonder what specific part of the brain is beneath my fingers. Which part is responsible for what's happening right now? I'm afraid I've unlocked something that I won't ever be able to ignore again.

I help Gram find her keys, and she finally snaps out of her daze.

"Thank you," she says to Mr. Rodriguez. "I think we'll be fine now."

He opens his mouth to say something but shuts it when Gram frowns at him in that way she has. Even befuddled, she has a dignity that makes you trust her. He nods and heads back to the truck.

I help buckle Clay into his car seat. Gram looks down at the key in her hand for several seconds before she finally turns it in the ignition. A gust of hot air hits us in the face, and I quickly adjust the vent to face away from her.

"You okay, Gram?"

"I'm fine," she says, but her voice shakes as she backs out of the parking space. I watch her carefully as she drives around the lot, searching for the nearest exit. She squints at the signs, rubbing her eyes as if her sight is the problem.

"This one." I point to where she should turn. She obeys with a small cluck of her tongue. It's the sound we use on the horses to soothe them, to let them know they don't need to worry.

Click. The day Gram moved in with us two years and six months ago. *Click.* What I wore that day, how she made me feel, what the weather was like. *Click.*

The day Gram forgot Clay's grilled cheese sandwich on the stove and the fire department had to come. *Click.* The way Gram looked at me with growing alarm for a whole minute last week, as if she didn't know who I was. As if I were a stranger.

2.

The Brain

Some things I know about the brain: it's pink, it's about the size of a head of cauliflower, and it weighs around three pounds for the average adult. Our brains won't allow us to tickle ourselves—it predicts the sensation and cancels the response to our own touch. It also generates enough electricity to power a light bulb.

If I found this information with one quick search on my phone, what will a more thorough study of the brain uncover? I can find why my memory upgraded and maybe even discover what's making Gram lose hers.

When we get home, Mom's in the kitchen with Dad, laughing while they make dinner together. This is how they've been since Gram moved in with us. They're still busy, but they smile more, spend time together. The sadness is still there, but it's not all the time; it only leaks out every now and then.

One of my first memories is of my baby sister, Maisie. Dad doesn't believe I really remember her. He says I was too young. But I remember missing the way Maisie stared up at me like she knew what I was thinking. I remember the night she died without any warning—when the ambulance came and my parents cried and cried. I remember not understanding why Mom wouldn't play with me anymore, why she stopped looking at me altogether.

Dad told me I needed to stop talking about Maisie in front of Mom, that it upset her too much. To him, my mom's happiness is the most important thing. It's bigger than mine or Clay's or even his own. He doesn't understand that to someone with my memory, the sorrow of the first day is always there. It bleeds across time and fills every crack of every day afterward. It stays with me no matter how much I try to get rid of it. How can you get over loss if it doesn't ever fade?

When Gram first moved in with us, I told her about Maisie and the night she died. She listened patiently as I told her that memory and so many more. She didn't shake her head and explain why they couldn't be real.

I'd been too young to know exact dates, but I could keep track of the days from when the ambulance came. I could remember that the bell down the street rang twelve times the morning after—which made it a Sunday. That I didn't know how to read yet but I knew my letters—which made me three. I could remember how the sun beat down on my head when I sat outside but the breeze was icy—which made it winter. How Dad took apart the hand-painted crib and wept when I asked him to make me lunch. How to this day, whenever he fixes me a sandwich, I worry he might cry again.

Gram pursed her lips when I told her all this. "You have an extraordinary memory, Lulu," she said. "Amazing, really. Have you told your parents?"

I thought she could make my parents understand. But not soon after, I overheard Dad and her arguing. "She was too young to remember that, Mom. She was barely three when it happened. We have enough on our plates without you filling her head with nonsense."

When Gram tucked me in later that night, she kissed my forehead. "Some people can only see their own sadness," she whispered. "One day they'll be ready. In the meantime, you tell me. You can tell me anything."

That was enough for me. I didn't need everyone to see me. It was enough that she did.

And now the house is filled with laughter again. Mom plays with Clay instead of acting like he doesn't exist. She and Dad listen to us talk with a lightness I hadn't realized I missed.

But I can't forget how easy it was for them to turn away and act like Clay and I weren't there. If the brain can predict when we're going to tickle ourselves, then shouldn't it also predict when we know we're about to get hurt and cancel out that reaction too? How can we protect ourselves if our brains won't let us?

"Get anything good at the mall?" Dad's wide grin crinkles the skin around his eyes with genuine humor. Olivia says he's handsome like Josh Duhamel, but I don't see it. He's way too goofy. He's always doing things like going on weird diets where all he eats are beets for three days and then bingeing on ice cream when he's finished. Mom says she loves him with extra weight, but I don't think he believes her.

"What's wrong with Clay?" Mom rushes forward and swoops Clay up in her arms.

Gram starts to explain. "I was a little—"

"Nothing," I say. "It's just really hot out and Gram's tired. Why don't you lie down, Gram? I'll bring you some water." Before she can say another word, I grab her hand and head down the hallway.

I glance behind us to make sure we weren't followed. "Gram, I don't think you should tell them about the parking lot. Remember how worried Dad got after the fire?"

Gram's normally clear blue eyes are bloodshot, and lipstick has settled in the wrinkles around her mouth. I concentrate on the neatly made bed in the background instead. The tightly tucked corners and perfectly placed throw pillows are who my grandmother is. Not this confused woman.

She straightens her blouse and pats the droopy white curls curved about the tops of her ears. "Your father is a good son and he loves me. I've taught him to never turn your back on family."

I wrinkle my nose. I don't share her confidence. "Maybe he'll stop worrying if you let him make you a doctor's appointment."

Gram waves her hand in dismissal. "I hate doctors. They give you medicine you don't need, and they'll say you're sick when you're not."

"But you're not going to talk about today, right?"

"I won't say anything," she says. "You know I am fine, yes?"

I don't know any such thing. Lately, when she

gets tired, her voice changes. She sounds like the lady in a movie we had to watch for history class. Is there a disease that gives you an accent?

She kisses my cheek and gives me a quick hug. I look past her to the old trunk pushed against the window. A memory whirls and opens. *Click.*

Soon after she moved in, on February 17, a Tuesday, Gram showed me this trunk. "Inside this treasure chest is a very special book about a girl who moved from far away. One day, when I am gone, it will be yours."

I used to think she'd only give me the book if she moved. And since I never wanted her to leave, I put it out of my mind. But now I wonder if the book might tell me more about Gram. I don't really know anything about when she was young. It's hard to imagine her ever being my age.

Is the book still in the chest? Is Gram the girl in the book? The questions prod at me, and for a moment, I forget how scared I'd been at the mall.

"I will take a nap and be as good as new, yes?" Gram's smile doesn't reassure me like it usually does.

She's speaking with that strange accent again.

Until today I thought Gram's forgetfulness would get better, that she was just tired or needed more help with Clay. She'd forget for a few seconds, or sometimes minutes, and then be fine again. This time she hadn't remembered for more than an hour.

I close the door softly behind me, and I hear Mom's and Dad's hushed voices filter down the hall. Avoiding the creaky floorboards, I tiptoe closer to the kitchen.

"I know," Dad says. "I made an appointment for next week. It might be nothing, but something isn't quite right."

"And have you noticed how she suddenly sounds like a supervillain in *Rocky and Bullwinkle*?" Mom's voice gets louder as she turns the faucet on.

"Dementia can present itself in all sorts of ways."

"So you think it's *Alzheimer's*?" Mom asks in the hushed voice she usually uses to talk about Maisie. I inch closer, holding my breath as I listen.

"No. She's probably just tired. She's getting older and refuses to slow down. Maybe she needs more rest, but I don't think we should rule anything out." Dad sounds sad, but I'm not fooled by it. If he was so sad, then he wouldn't have had a brochure for a place called Pleasant Oaks Retirement Home on his desk.

When I found the brochure yesterday, I crumpled it up, like if Dad couldn't see it, he might forget.

My mind races. I can't blindly trust my parents to make the right decision. They've shown me what they do when life gets too hard to handle. Dad runs to work, and Mom shuts herself away in her art studio. Everyone and everything else is ignored.

I can't let Gram go into a home. I can't imagine my life without her in it.

I sneak away to my room to look up Alzheimer's. Each paragraph of information is stored safely away. Some I understand, others I don't. *Click.* I won't forget. I can't.

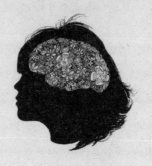

3.

Temporal Lobe

People with HSAM have brains that are different from most everyone else's. There's a part in their brain called the temporal lobe that's bigger. Which makes sense, since the temporal lobe is where we store memories. They say they can find the cure for Alzheimer's by studying people who have HSAM. They hope to reverse engineer the process of how these kinds of memories work so they can prevent memory disorders and maybe even cure them.

* * *

Today at the mall my brain showed a glimpse of what it can do, of what it's been hinting at for a while. I used to think I might have an eidetic memory or a photographic memory, but I've ruled that out after this afternoon. After scouring the Internet, I'm pretty sure I have what's known as a highly superior autobiographical memory.

There's a doctor who studies people with HSAM. He says people with this kind of memory can recall almost every day of their lives in amazing detail, as well as public events that hold personal meaning to them. They can "see" a vivid picture of each day in their heads.

I test myself by looking at old class pictures from three years ago. Now that I've stopped trying to ignore it, my memory clicks on quickly. Where I saw the map earlier, a 3-D calendar pops up in the air in front of me. I can "see" pictures on each of the dates—little clues about what happened that day.

Click. I pick a calendar square, pulling it out and opening it up. It unravels, with each detail playing out in front of me. I'm back in the classroom, with the faint smell of Mr. Guerro's cologne mixing with the musty aroma of our class's pet guinea pig, Marbles. I remember what each of my friends was wearing that day, down to their shoes and backpacks.

I immediately know why this particular day stands out. It was right after Clay was born, when Mom went from sad to never getting out of bed.

I felt alone at home. I didn't want to be alone at school, too.

So I tried extra hard to fit in and be liked. I smiled more, laughed at jokes even if they weren't funny. And, of course, I copied how the most popular girl in class dressed. On this day my green sweater exactly matched one Piper wore the previous year.

Piper almost never wore something twice. But that day she did.

"Look, Piper!" Megan said with a smile that was a little too wide. "You and Lulu are wearing the same thing."

"I bought it last weekend," I said.

"So did I," Piper said with a forced laugh, her

glare fixed and present. She slung her arm across my shoulder and posed with her head next to mine. "Who wore it best?"

"No. You bought it last year," I reminded her. "You wore it six months ago, right before spring break. It was April fifteenth and it was a Friday, the day we went on a field trip to see the play of *Fiddler on the Roof.*"

Piper's mouth fell open. She pulled away so fast, I thought she might topple over. "What are you, some kind of stalker? Do you, like, take pictures of everything I wear and write it in your stalker diary?"

Megan snorted. "Good one, Piper. Lulu's stalker diary."

Several girls giggled and whispered behind their hands. My face burned hotter than the asphalt outside. Olivia saved me. She put both hands on her hips and rolled her eyes. "Oh, please. Lulu's hopeless with clothes. We all know that. It's a *compliment* that she wanted to copy you, Piper. And we all know you've worn that sweater before. It's too cute for any of us to forget, duh."

Piper flipped her hair and sniffed. "I don't know if you want to hang out with a stalker, Olivia. What will everyone think? They might think you're a stalker too."

Megan and the others nodded and turned their backs on me. Olivia linked her arm though mine and walked toward the playground, but she kept looking back at Piper and her gang.

I knew then that I had to keep my memory a secret. I'd be a weirdo, a stalker, a complete outsider if anyone found out. So I shut down my memory as much as I could, and what I couldn't shut down I kept to myself. I didn't even tell Olivia. I know she'd never make fun of me, but being popular is important to her. She cares what other girls, especially Piper, think of her. Would she still be friends with me if she had to choose between us? Maybe. But I didn't want to take that chance.

So I told no one until Gram.

But now there's no more holding my memory back. I can feel it, like something charged with electricity sparking in my brain. What if people find out?

What if no one will ever talk to me again? What if Olivia decides I'm too weird to hang around with?

Max looked at me like I was a freak when I remembered where the van was. Although, to be fair, that's how he usually looks at me. I can only imagine how much he'd tease me if he knew the whole truth. It would be worse than when he teased me for a whole month after I wore the wrong riding boots. Or the time I put Remy's halter on wrong. Or when I forgot to tighten my saddle and nearly fell off. Max's laugh is the reason I double-check my saddle to this day.

If Max found out about my memory, he would make my life a nightmare. I could never go back to the stables, and I don't know what I'd do if I couldn't ride. Encouraging me to ride was another gift of Gram's. And when she saw how much I loved it, she talked Dad into buying Remy for me.

I study every story on the Internet about people who have HSAM. Their stories make me feel a little less alone, and it's amazing to hear how similar my memory is to theirs. Most didn't even know their memories were different until they were about my age, so at least I'm normal in this area of my life. One woman said her memory grew each year, until she could remember every second of a day in the blink of an eye.

It feels strange to read about scientists studying the brains of people with HSAM. What are the odds I have the kind of memory that could help someone who is losing theirs? What if my memory actually holds the key to helping Gram?

I imagine myself strapped to a table with wires connecting my brain to Gram's. I would give Gram all of my memory—every bit—if it kept her from forgetting me. I never want to see her look right through me like she did last Wednesday. Not ever again.

It happened right when it was time to drive me to my riding lesson. Gram had just locked the front door. The keys slipped from her hands and fell on the porch, so I scooped them up and handed them back.

"Why am I here?" Gram asked, looking from the keys in her hand to me. She stared at me blankly, frowning like she didn't trust me. Like I was a bug crawling across the floor. A bug she didn't recognize.

A pulse drummed against my forehead. "To take me to riding," I answered.

I was used to how Mom looked past me, as if she were seeing another little girl from another time and place. Or how Dad kept his eyes glued to his phone, pausing to glance at Clay or me with an absent-minded smile. They love me, but they don't see me. A piece of their heart is locked away—maybe forever. But with Gram, Clay and I have her whole heart. Every part of us is important to her.

Except now Gram's brows stayed furrowed. Her cheeks turned pink, and then a bright red stained her neck and chest. "I know you?"

"It's Lulu," I said, not sure if I was reminding her or myself. Who was I if I didn't have Gram on my side? Her voice was with me always. Telling me how special I was, how brave, how beautiful. An empty space under my ribs opened up. It tugged on my heart like it was trying to pull it out of place and swallow it whole.

"Lulu," she repeated in a whisper. "Lulu. Yes."

The moment she snapped back, her eyes locked on me like lasers. And the empty space under my ribs closed right back up.

It was nothing. I repeated that over and over every day since.

She was tired and I'd only imagined it.

But then she burned Clay's sandwich and forgot where we parked at the mall. And a dozen other small things piled one on top of another. Little nothings that became one big something.

4.

Hippo Brain

There's a small part of the brain called the hippocampus, which makes me imagine a hippopota-
mus stomping around in the middle of my skull.
That would explain why memories are so random.
Why you remember some and not others.

Only, the hippocampus doesn't look a thing like
a hippo. It's shaped like a seahorse, and it helps us
remember things like where our home is. Something
that might seem easy.

One of the first symptoms of Alzheimer's is

forgetting where things are. Maybe at first it's where you park. Pretty soon it's something more, maybe even people. There's no cure for it yet. Once you get it, you start losing your memory in bits and pieces until eventually you don't remember anyone or anything.

I plop down at the kitchen table and grab a home-made blueberry muffin. Gram bakes the best muffins. "I have a plan," I say, and I take a humongous bite that slowly melts in my mouth.

Gram cuts up a pear for Clay, each slice as precise and efficient as she is. Her hair is curled, her makeup perfect, everything just so. Maybe I'm worrying too much. Maybe yesterday was just a bad day.

"I'm sure you do." A faint smile softens the stern lines of her face.

When Gram first moved in with us, I was a little afraid of her. Everything about her seemed rigid and strict. But she'd won me over within days—she never forgot to pick me up, she always did what she said, and she didn't just say she loved me. She showed it.

Gram knew my teachers' names and Olivia's favorite snack. She read to Clay and me, told us stories about Dad when he was young. And she listened to me. Nothing I said bored her or made her impatient.

While Mom locked herself away in her studio, Gram took me to riding lessons and doted on Clay. She saved our whole family—couldn't Mom and Dad see that? Why would they want to move her to a retirement home?

I try to stay calm. "You need to tell me everything you remember," I tell her. "I'll record it. That way if you forget something, I can give the memory back to you."

I pull out a notebook and pen. There's something soothing about writing things down, where everything has a place, orderly and neat. It unclutters my brain, at least for a little while. Ever since yesterday, a smell or a picture might catapult me back in time to a specific moment. If I'm going to learn to control it, maybe writing things down can be the first step.

Gram wipes her hands as she considers my proposition. "Everything? That's a lot of memories, yes? Are you sure you want to waste the rest of your summer listening to my old stories?"

"I want to," I assure her, forcing a smile. "It'll be fun."

"Are you feeling okay?" She tilts her head as she studies my face. Her eyes scan me like she has X-ray vision. Sometimes I'm half convinced she does.

My leg jiggles underneath the table. "I'm fine."

"Is this about yesterday? I told you not to worry about me. Everyone gets a little forgetful every once in a while." She reaches out and fixes my bangs so they don't cover my eyes.

I, on the other hand, like when they cover my eyes. A thick curtain of hair to hide what I'm really thinking. "I just think it would be cool to know more about your past. You know everything about me."

Gram smiles, her eyes twinkling with humor. "Yes, this is true. I know that the boy yesterday makes you very angry. Why?"

I sigh. I should have seen this coming. Every time Gram sees Max at the stables, she smiles like she knows something I don't. "Just because *you* think Max is cute doesn't mean I do. He's annoying and a know-it-all."

"But also very sweet. It says something about him that he was so patient with an old lady."

I shrug. "I guess he was sort of nice to you—"

"He was more than nice, Lulu. He was a gentleman." She smiles again like she expects me to declare my love for Max Rodriguez.

Yeah, *so* not going to happen.

"Can we not talk about Max for a second, and go back to your stories? I want to know about your childhood. Who was your best friend? When did you first start riding horses? Things like that."

"I am happy you want to know me, my sweet girl. But I think you are also a little afraid for me, yes?"

I look away from her all-knowing gaze. "Maybe a little."

"I've been putting some thought into going to the doctor," Gram says. "Perhaps if I make an appointment myself, with a friend of mine? That way everyone can rest assured that I am perfectly fine."

"Who is it?"

She fiddles with her scarf and glances out the window. "No one you know. We go way back. After we have a quick talk, he will see I am well and will e-mail your father."

"He won't want to examine you?" Things are sounding fishier by the minute.

"That isn't necessary. Like I said earlier, I'm fine. Just a little tired, yes?"

I know there's more wrong than a little tiredness, and something feels off about this doctor's visit. But Gram's always been honest with me. "I guess if you're sure he knows what he's doing."

"He does, and he knows me well. Not like a strange doctor who thinks they know everything about you from one test."

I wiggle my pencil. "Fine. But I do really want to know more about you, Gram, and not just because I'm worried. Like, what's your earliest memory?"

Instead of answering, Gram goes to the small radio she keeps by the sink. "I think it's time for a dance party. What do you think, Clay?"

"Dance!" Clay pounds his tray with both fists.

Gram turns the radio on, and a Beatles song fills the room. She starts to shimmy to the beat. "Come on, Lulu. Show me those moves!"

I roll my eyes and giggle when she does a weird dance where it looks like she's swimming. Gram has been dancing every day with us since she moved here. Sometimes we even get Mom and Dad to join us if we play the right eighties song.

Gram grabs my hands and twirls me until I laugh breathlessly. I forget to be self-conscious once my feet start moving to the music. Clay demands to get down so he can be a part of it too, and soon we're all dancing in a circle. Gram takes turns spinning us and shows Clay how to do the twist.

The first song ends and another that has an even catchier beat starts. Three songs later, Gram leans against the counter with a chuckle. "Okay, sweet boy, that's enough dancing for now. We need to get you upstairs for a nap."

Clay shakes his head and runs around the kitchen in increasingly smaller circles.

I hold my stomach and laugh. "He's never going to sleep now."

"Dance party rules," Gram says with a smile as she turns the music down. "Big boys must take their naps or no more dancing later on. You don't want that, do you?"

Clay stops in his tracks and puts his hands up. "Nap, Gwam."

Gram pats the top of my head before moving to wipe Clay's hands with a washcloth. "You two are the best things in my life," she says. "You do realize that, Lulu?"

"Yes, Gram." My feet tap to the music still playing softly in the background.

Gram picks Clay up and kisses his bright red cheek. "Why don't we start with my stories after I put him down for a nap? I have the best story about your dad at your age."

It's strange to think of Dad as a child. He's such a grown-up, and there's nothing that would hint he was once ever anything but a history professor.

"I think we should start with *your* childhood

growing up in San Francisco," I say. "Then work our way up."

In all my reading, one article gave me hope that what Gram has might be curable. It said that sometimes someone becomes forgetful because of a traumatic memory. Something your brain *wants* to forget, so it forgets everything.

Maybe—just maybe—if I can find that memory, then I can help fix Gram's forgetfulness.

I know it's a long shot, but sometimes extraordinary things can happen. I was alone and invisible for years. Fed, clothed, but passed over like a forgotten sock behind the dryer. Gram swept in with her rules and practicality. She opened the blinds and let sunshine spill in to help find the part of me that was lost.

I can't have this highly superior autobiographical memory for no reason. I must have it to solve this puzzle. If there's the smallest chance a traumatic memory from Gram's past is the reason she's losing her memory, then I owe it to science and to Gram to rule it out.

"Gram," I say, "what was your childhood like?"

Gram's lips tremble, and her eyes glisten. "I'd rather not talk about that. Some things should stay in the past."

5.

Limbic System

The part of the brain that creates memories is found in the limbic system. Sometimes something happens where a person can't remember huge chunks of their life. In most cases, they're diagnosed with dissociative amnesia. Usually it's because something happens that's so bad, the brain shuts off the memory to protect itself. Brain scans of patients with this kind of amnesia show they can't remember emotional memories, no matter how hard they try. The traumatic memory changes the actual structure of the brain.

* * *

Gram doesn't want to talk about her childhood, and just mentioning it upsets her. *I knew it!* Gram doesn't have Alzheimer's at all! There's a memory in her past she's buried so deep, it's making her forgetful. If I can help her find the traumatic memory, then everything will be fine.

"But . . ." I search for a reason that might reach her. "I trusted you with my secret. Don't you trust me with yours?"

"Of course," Gram says, shifting Clay to her other hip. "But I would rather remember happy things. That is better I think, yes?"

"What about the book in your treasure chest?" I ask. The words slip out before I can stop myself.

Gram stops and turns around, the lower half of her face hidden behind Clay's head. "What book?"

"The one you showed me when you first moved here. You said it was about a girl from far away. Is it about you? Are you the girl from far away?"

"I don't know of any book," Gram says in a shaky

voice. "If you'll excuse me, I need to go put your brother down."

She spins around and rushes out of the room faster than I've ever seen her move. Clay waves sleepily over Gram's shoulder as she practically runs up the stairs. I raise my hand to wave back while my mind races. Dad always said Gram's mom and dad were the best grandparents ever, so why doesn't Gram want to talk about when she was young?

And what about the book? Did she forget it, or is she lying? I *know* there's a story there, and it could hold the key to understanding what's happening to her now. What if I took a peek at it without her knowing?

I pace down the hallway and then back. *I can't snoop in Gram's personal things. She'd never trust me again.*

But . . . the Gram I know is slipping away. No matter how many times I tell myself she's just tired, I know it's more. I know it's serious. What if this book is the only way I can help her?

When Gram goes to Clay's room, I tiptoe to hers. I hesitate outside the door. Invading her privacy doesn't feel right, but how else can I help her? I can't do one without the other. Besides, she said she would give me the book one day. In a way she's sort of given me permission.

I narrow my eyes at the old chest pushed against the far wall. A white lace tablecloth flows evenly down either side, with four giant stacks of books piled precisely on top. The cloth only just hides the battered wood of the chest.

It looks ancient. Just like a treasure chest.

Clay's voice filters down the stairs. He always begs for an extra story. It'll take at least half an hour for him to fall asleep, which is plenty of time to take a peek. I don't need to read the whole thing—just enough to ask her the right kinds of questions.

I stack the books on the floor and push the tablecloth off. But when I try to lift the hinge, the lid doesn't budge. I kneel down and notice a small keyhole underneath the latch.

My gaze darts around the room, searching for a key, before coming to rest on my pottery clamshell on the window ledge. I made it for Gram two years ago, and she keeps it filled with buttons, safety pins, pennies, and random keys.

I try three of the keys before one works. *Yes!* My chest burns, and I let out a sigh of relief. The lid creaks open and I hold my breath, half convinced there might be gold hidden beneath piles of gems.

But there's no gold. The chest falls open to reveal more books and some old papers. A plain black book with a gold lock rests on top.

Is this the book I need? I remember it being bigger.

I search the clamshell for a smaller key that might fit, but they're all too big. I'm running out of time—Clay has stopped talking, and I can hear my heart beating in the complete quiet of the house.

I set the book aside and concentrate on putting everything back the way I found it. I have no choice but to take the book with me. I'll find a way to open it, read what I need, and then put it back later. I doubt Gram ever looks in the chest, so it should be safe to keep it for a day or so.

The sound of her voice calling me from the kitchen makes me jump.

I run to the doorway and turn back to do a quick once-over. Nothing seems out of place. I head down the hall and tuck the book into my backpack before I answer.

"Here, Gram."

She frowns, and I hold my breath. Does she suspect? I've never been able to hide things from her. She always senses when something's wrong. But she has no way of knowing I've been in her room, does she? I wait for her to ask where I've been and why I look so guilty.

Instead, she opens the refrigerator and grabs the milk. Her hands are steady as she pours a huge glass and pushes it toward me. "Are you ready for the story about your dad?"

"I don't drink milk," I say, hesitant to correct her. Is she testing me? Can she tell I have the book?

"Oh yes." Her mouth puckers for a second before she smiles. "I'll drink it. Am I taking you riding today?"

She's getting that empty look in her eyes again, and something in my chest tightens. "Later in the afternoon. After Clay wakes up," I remind her.

She wrinkles her nose at the glass in her hands. "Why am I drinking this? I hate milk."

"You don't have to drink it, Gram."

She sets it down inside the sink and starts to wipe the already spotless counter.

"Gram, do you really not remember the book you showed me when you first moved here?" I ask. The same book burning a hole in my backpack this very second.

She blinks, her eyes going blank. "Where is your brother?"

"He's taking a nap." I bite my lip with worry. Is she forgetting because I asked about the book? Did just thinking about it make her memory worse?

"Oh yes!" She smiles, her eyes softening. "He hates naps."

"Gram," I press. I hate to bring it up again, but how will I find out if I don't ask? "Are you the girl from far away?"

She shakes her head. Her lip trembles, and I'm afraid she might cry. "I don't want to talk about her."

"Okay." I smile reassuringly, but I feel like I'm failing her somehow. "Do you want to tell me the story about Dad?"

She nods, the panic in her eyes fading. I only half-listen as she tells me a story I've heard a hundred times before.

My mind drifts to the book tucked in my backpack. My feet tap, my legs twitch, and my hands pluck at my shorts until I can't take it any longer.

"I need to do something, Gram. I'll be right back."

"Oh, of course." Gram waves a hand in front of her face. "Here I am blabbing away when you need to get ready. Go ahead. I'll just tidy up the kitchen. Clay should be up soon, and then we'll be off to the mall. We need to get you those riding boots."

"Yes." I don't correct her and say we bought them yesterday and that we're going to the stables and not the mall. I need to see what's in the book.

I shut myself in my room and search for something to pick the lock. I try the Swiss Army knife Dad gave me after he and Mom came back from a trip. After half an hour, I'm a sweaty mess and no closer to opening it. How do thieves do it? The lock looks flimsy, but looks are deceiving.

My phone buzzes a few times in a row while I'm turning the book over in my hands. Olivia's text messages usually come in threes. She can't grasp the concept of one long text when three or four short ones are so much more dramatic.

Olivia: Guess who is teaching

Olivia: class at the stables?

Olivia: You will never guess.

An idea hits me. Last month she'd jimmied the bathroom door lock when her baby cousin locked herself in.

Me: Do you know how to pick locks?

Olivia: Of course.

Olivia: Why?

Olivia: Max is teaching!! Are we happy for him or mad?

Me: I need you to pick a lock for me. It's on a book. And what????????? Why is he teaching??? He's our age!! How is that OK???

Olivia: His dad told him he'd give him a shot at

teaching after he turned thirteen. You know Mr. R will be watching Max like a hawk.

Olivia: I can pick it

Olivia: Bring it today.

Olivia: See you later

With Max teaching my riding class, the day promises to stink more than manure. What if he says something about what happened at the mall? Will he make fun of Gram in front of everyone? I rub the ache between my ribs harder than necessary.

I put on my riding clothes and stare at the book. Its dark cover is old with cracks burrowed deep into the leather. What secrets does it hold? I tuck it into my backpack and jog down the stairs to see if Gram's ready to take me to the stables.

I find Gram sitting on the couch staring blankly at the wall. I walk closer, careful not to startle her.

"Are you ready?" I ask softly.

She blinks as if to bring me into focus, and I can tell she's trying to work out what we're supposed to be doing. I push down on my chest and breathe past the building pressure. "You're going to drive me to the stables. Do you want me to get Clay?"

"Lulu," she says slowly. A light turns back on. "Oh, sweetie. I'm sorry. Yes, can you fetch the little guy? I'll get a snack for him."

I make sure she reaches the kitchen before I run up to get Clay. I carry him downstairs and buckle him into his car seat. Gram smiles at me as she starts the van; the blank look of a few minutes ago is gone, but the pain in my chest is still there.

I think about the book in my backpack, its secrets locked up tight. Like Gram's memories, waiting for me to break them free.

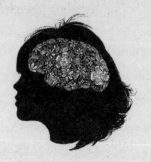

6.

Gone with the Cerebellum

The word "cerebellum" sounds like one of those big Southern mansions, like in Gram's favorite movie, *Gone with the Wind*. The cerebellum is the part of the brain that's in charge of keeping our balance and coordination. It helps maintain our posture and fine motor skills, which can be easy to take for granted. Until something you can usually do effortlessly apparently isn't good enough for your riding instructor. And he makes you look like an idiot.

* * *

"Chin up," Max calls out. "Don't look down, Lulu."

I can barely hear him above the pounding of my heart. Why is he picking on me? I know I'm not the best rider here, but there are six other girls and I'm the only one he's corrected the whole lesson. It doesn't help that Mr. Rodriguez watches quietly from the sidelines.

Olivia looks worried when she meets my gaze. *Sorry*, she mouths, making a face.

"Okay, let's call it," Max shouts, whacking the side of his boot with the riding crop. "Finish up, and don't forget to groom your own horses. If you love them, show them."

"Harsh," Piper says loudly. She's been trying to get his attention the whole lesson, and he's barely said one word to her.

"But true," he says. "Last lesson I had to groom all five horses. Not my job."

"Pretty sure it is," Piper says, tossing her perfectly curled hair. "My mom pays your dad to do that for us." She hands him her horse's reins and stomps off.

"Lulu and I always groom our own horses," Olivia says, glaring at Piper's back.

"Good for you," he says, and I can't tell if he's being sarcastic. He nods to me and saunters off with Piper's horse.

"He did okay today," Olivia whispers as we lead our horses back to the barn. "He was kind of tough on you, though."

Remy nudges me with his nose. I lean against him briefly. "I guess."

"I can tell him he was a jerk if you want me to," she offers.

"No, it's fine," I say with a sigh. "He was right. I do need to keep my chin up."

Olivia puts both hands on her hips. "Whatever. Next time he's mean to you, I'll show him how to keep *his* chin up."

I shake my head. Now that class is over, Max is no longer important. I change the subject to what's been on my mind the whole lesson. "I brought the book with the lock."

"The one you need me to break into? Anything I should know about?"

"It's an old book I found," I say with a shrug.

"You know how I am with mysteries."

Olivia takes a rubber curry brush out of the bucket. "You like books too much in general."

I ignore this and grab my backpack. I pull the book out carefully. "Here it is."

"Ooh." Olivia snatches the book from my hands and holds it reverently. "This looks super old! Where did you find it?"

"Nowhere special. Just tucked away."

"Hmmm." Olivia puts the lock up to the light. "It seems simple enough."

"Don't break it, though. I don't want the pages ripping or anything."

"Chill, little Lulu. I'm a master at this kind of thing." She pulls a bobby pin out of her hair and strips the end off with her teeth. She bends it until it's one long, thin piece of metal before jiggling it into the lock. "The trick is to get it sharp enough and feel for the little thingy to click."

I wait while she fiddles with it, her hair falling over her face and hiding the book from me. She makes a sound of triumph and holds the open book up in the air. "Ta-da! I'm a genius, y'all."

"You are!" I laugh with relief. "Hand it over."

"I wanna look," she says, sitting on an overturned bucket. "I did all the hard work."

I try to tamp down the impulse to rip it out of her hand, and I pull another bucket over. She tilts the book in my direction and hesitates before opening it. Even Olivia seems to feel the weight of the moment.

She flips to the first page, revealing what at first looks to be a bunch of scribbles. A jumble of curved letters swoop across the thin paper.

"What is this?" I mumble. Is it in code?

"I think it's the Cyrillic alphabet," Olivia says. "My cousins are from Serbia, and that's what their language looks like."

Why would Gram's book be in another language? I've never even heard of Cyrillic. I clutch the book so tight, the tips of my fingers turn white.

"Thanks for opening it." I close it and slip it into my backpack. Remy blows out air softly through his nostrils, drawing my attention back to him. He sniffs, wondering where his treat is.

Olivia pouts. "I wanted to read what was in it. Now we'll never know what it says."

"I'll have to find out what language it is," I say.

"I know what you can do!" She holds up her phone. "You can totally change the keyboard on your phone and compare the different Cyrillic ones. See which one looks the closest. I can help, if you want."

"How do I change it?" I ask.

"Go to Settings, General, and then Keyboard." She leans over my shoulder as I follow her directions. "Try Serbian first."

I pick Serbian and examine the symbols. "It's hard to tell if it's the right one. I bet I can use Google Translate."

"Try it," she urges.

"We need to finish with the horses." I tuck my phone in my pocket. "I'll try again later and let you know what I find out."

"I love solving stuff," Olivia says, pulling a carrot out of her satchel and feeding it to her horse, Brandy. "A book written in another language abandoned at your house. Why don't things like that ever happen to me?"

My imagination goes wild as I think of all the reasons why Gram would have a journal written in another language. Olivia and I groom our horses in silence for a few more minutes before Max shows up.

"Thanks. I'll take it from here," he says. "Your grandmother feeling better, Lulu?"

Heat floods my cheeks, and I avoid Olivia's questioning look. "Yes. Thanks for your help."

"Help?" Olivia squeaks. "What help?"

Max takes in my wide eyes for a second before turning to Olivia. "I hear you might enter the next jumping competition. I think you've got a good shot at placing. Let me know if you want extra time in the arena."

Olivia's mouth opens and closes. "Sure, okay, thanks."

Max nods before heading toward his dad's office. He knew exactly what to say to distract Olivia. She's completely forgotten to be mad at him and chatters excitedly about the competition while we wait in front of the barn to be picked up.

I'm also sort of surprised that Max kept quiet about Gram. He could have made fun of her—of me—but he didn't.

"I bet if I add another lesson on the weekend, it would totally help me get ready. What do you think?" Olivia asks.

Before I can answer, Piper stomps out of the barn and drops her bag so close to my foot, the strap whips my leg. "Ugh, I can't believe the babysitter drove her own clunker when my mom told her she can drive the Audi. So apparently it broke down and I have to, like, wait. Can I just catch a ride, Olivia?"

Olivia glances at me from the corner of her eye. "Um, sure!"

Piper flashes me a tight smile. "Seems like Max had it out for you today. Give people power and they turn into complete jerks, right?"

"He was just doing his job," I say, the words tumbling out of my mouth. *Since when do I defend Max Rodriguez?*

Piper sniffs and turns her back on me to face

Olivia. "I was wondering if we can stop off at this little shop on the way to my house? Their ice cream is so completely amazing. It will change your life."

Olivia laughs as if Piper is the funniest person in the world. "I love ice cream!" She leans around Piper so she can see me. "What about you, Lulu? You want to get some ice cream with us?"

I try to return Olivia's smile. "If you're talking about the ice cream shop on the corner of Fourth Street, they're closed for the next two weeks. They go out of town this time every year."

"They were just open yesterday," Piper says, whipping her head around to give me her famous glare.

"They always close from the third weekend of June to the first weekend of July," I say. There's no way I'm giving in to Piper when I know I'm right. There's something satisfying about proving her wrong.

Piper's eyes narrow. "Is there a sign on the shop window or something?"

"No," I answer.

"Then how do you know?" She folds her arms

and nods to Olivia like she's proving a point.

Olivia turns to me and waits for my answer. For the logical explanation Piper somehow knows I won't have.

"The owner told me," I say, feeling like I can't take a deep enough breath. I understand what Piper's trying to do. She wants to make me look ridiculous in front of my best friend. Piper's poisoned everyone else against me; it's only a matter of time before Olivia listens to her too.

"When did the owner tell you?" Piper's smile is all teeth and pink lip gloss.

I slowly close my fingers into a fist and squeeze it tight. "Last year before they left."

"And you remembered all this time?" Piper asks, her eyes wide with fake shock. "Do you stalk them, too? Is there anyone you don't stalk?"

There's a pile of horse manure behind Piper. I bet her shiny boots have never once touched any kind of poop, and for one brief second I fantasize about changing that.

"Remembering when an ice cream store closes

isn't stalking them," Olivia says. I glance at her gratefully, but she avoids my gaze and bites her thumbnail. If Olivia sees me differently after the smallest glimpse of my memory, what will happen if she finds out the whole truth?

"Whatever," Piper says, picking up her purse. "There's your mom, Olivia. If the ice cream place is closed, you can come over to my place for a swim." She turns and heads to Olivia's car without a glance at me.

"Later, Lulu." Olivia waves as she follows Piper, but she still won't look me in the eye.

I stare as they drive off, the dust from the road kicked up behind the car. With Gram slipping away, I won't have anyone else if Olivia stops being my friend too.

When Gram pulls up next to the barn, I try to shake off the sadness that covers me in a film of grit and dirt. She fiddles with the buttons by the steering wheel, her head bent as she tries to find the right one to unlock my door. I knock on her window until she rolls it down, and point to the button she's searching for.

She pushes it with a flustered laugh. "Oh, there it is. All these buttons are so confusing, yes?"

I don't reply as I throw my stuff on the floor next to Clay. My bag falls over and the book slides out. I shove it back inside with a quick glance at Gram, but her focus is on the road ahead.

My plan had been to go home and call Olivia so we could find the right language. But now I'm not sure what to do.

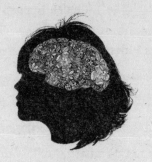

7.

Meninges

Just like a water filter protects us from drinking gross stuff, our meninges are made up of three membranes that protect our brain and spine: the pia layer, the arachnoid layer, and the dura layer, or PAD. These three layers "pad" the brain and spinal cord. They provide a supportive framework for the central nervous system and protect it. The more I think about it, the more I realize I have to be the meninges and protect Gram. No matter what it takes.

* * *

Gram smiles when I slip into the front seat of the van. "Good lesson?"

"Not bad. Max taught it. I guess he did okay."

"He's such a nice boy. Such good manners and so handsome."

"Mmm." I push away thoughts of Olivia and Piper and the hurt that bubbled up when Olivia refused to meet my eye. I have to be even more careful about hiding my secret. No one but Gram can ever know the real me. No one else would understand. And if she forgot who I was . . .

I *have* to find a way to keep that from happening.

Everything seems to lead back to the book. I could ask Gram what language it's written in, but I also don't want to set her off. Just talking about the book earlier seemed to make her memory worse.

"Gram, do you know another language?"

She glances at me, her eyebrows rising like they do when I ask for the sugar cereal she never lets me get. "Why?"

"Max . . . um . . . Max speaks Spanish fluently." Since she seems to think Max is the sweetest boy ever.

She smiles again. "Of course! He must have grown up speaking it. It will be natural for him."

"I was thinking about learning another language," I say. The lie tightens inside my throat. It feels like the time I drank milk and broke into hives.

"Perhaps Max will teach you some Spanish."

"Maybe." And maybe I'd rather shove toothpicks under my fingernails. Bad enough he's teaching my riding lessons with his know-it-all smirk. Being nice for one second doesn't automatically erase years of lording it over me.

"I always think it's good to know more than one language," Gram continues. "Most people in Europe know three or four. My mother could speak at least that many."

"I didn't know that," I say softly.

We pull up to the house, and Gram smiles wistfully. "She had a real ear for language. She always said one day she wanted to learn Chinese. Your great-grandfather used to say she could mimic any accent flawlessly."

"What was her first language?"

Gram looks over at me, but her eyes are out of focus. As if she sees something that isn't there.

"Gram?" I press. I don't want to push her too far, but I really need an answer.

Clay lets out a screech. "Out!" he yells, kicking his legs furiously against the back of the seat.

"Thanks a lot, brat," I mutter. Gram jerks out of her limbo and rushes around the side of the van to unbuckle him.

She kisses his cheek. "Let's get you inside, sweet boy." He starts to cry when she takes too long to unhook him. Gram mumbles to herself before stepping back and looking at me in confusion. "It's stuck."

I step around her and easily unsnap the buckle with one hand. Clay launches himself into my arms, and I permit his sloppy kisses as I carry him to the porch. He plops down on the welcome mat and waits as I take his shoes off.

"Lulu!" he shouts, and barrels inside. I kick off my boots on the porch and pad into the house in my socks.

"Oh good, you're home," Mom says, rushing

down the stairs. "I need to pop off to the store for ten minutes. Can you watch them, Sue?"

What does she think Gram's been doing all day? Her life is spent taking care of us.

Before Gram came, Mom would sometimes be too sad to even get out of bed. I can understand her sadness about the baby, but why did having Clay make her worse? Sometimes I think she uses her sadness as an excuse to stay away from us. As if Maisie were her one true child and Clay and I will never be enough.

Gram frowns faintly like she does when she's confused. My heart thumps hard. What if she has one of her forgetful episodes in front of Mom?

Mom slips her shoes on and grabs her purse. She waits for Gram's answer.

Gram opens her mouth, but I can see the confusion painted across her face, so I start to cough. I cough so loud, my throat hurts with it.

Mom steps backward. "Goodness, Lulu. Are you getting sick?"

"Allergies. I get them sometimes after I ride," I

say, moving to the door so Mom faces me and away from Gram. I've never had allergies, but Mom won't know that. She doesn't like to watch me ride. Her excuse is that she worries about me falling, but it's kind of hard to believe that when you add everything else together.

"Okay. Well, I'll be back in a bit. Did you need anything? I can get you those granola bars you like. The ones with the chocolate chips."

I hate granola bars and Clay won't eat anything with chocolate in it. But this isn't surprising, coming from Mom. "No, thanks," I say.

Mom checks her text messages before flashing me a distracted smile. "Okay, well, text me if you think of anything you might want." She squints over my shoulder to where Gram is helping Clay pick out books to read. Mom lowers her voice to a near whisper. "Keep an eye on Gram for me, okay? Let me know if she seems . . . not herself."

I fold both arms across my chest. "What do you mean?" I ask.

Mom waves a hand like she's painting the air.

"Oh, you know. If she gets too tired or confused."

I bite my tongue to keep from yelling. "Why do you say that?" My voice breaks and squeaks, like someone playing trumpet for the first time.

"Don't worry about it," Mom says, already halfway out the door. "Help her, okay?"

"I will, but she's fine. Seriously. I don't know why you're even saying that."

Mom glances back, her hand on the doorknob. "It's not a huge deal, Lulu. Dad's worried that she seems a little tired. But I'm happy to know you haven't noticed anything."

I nod and force a smile. "Yep. Gram's been great. She said she was going to make her famous lasagna tonight."

Mom tucks her thick hair behind one ear. "That sounds wonderful. I'll call your dad and let him know."

I lean against the closed door, my throat still scratchy from my faked coughing fit. I listen as Mom starts the car. What would happen if I told her and Dad the truth?

The Memory Keeper

I think of our family before Gram showed up—of Mom in bed all day, of Dad trying to keep us out of the way, of me doing my best to take care of Clay. I grit my teeth. They wouldn't help Gram if they knew the truth. They'd just have another reason to send her away. Away from me.

I have to hold them off for a little bit longer. Just until I find the memory that will fix Gram. And in the meantime, to show Mom and Dad that Gram is fine, I have to make sure she makes the best lasagna they've ever had.

I peek into the living room on my way to the kitchen. Gram and Clay are cuddled together on the couch, reading his favorite animal sounds book. The sound of Clay's moos follows me into the kitchen.

I pull out Gram's recipe book, the one with handwritten recipes filed behind pictures she's cut out of culinary magazines. The last time we made one of her recipes together, the measurements confused her and I had to take over. She sat in the chair with a cup of tea and watched as I crushed garlic and sautéed onions, and the smells seemed to wrap around me like a warm hug.

This time I prep all the ingredients. I chop the onions, tomatoes, and garlic and put the water on to boil. The egg-and-garlic mixture is folded inside the ricotta. My arms ache as I grate a mountain of mozzarella cheese. When I go get Gram, all she has to do is help me layer the lasagna.

"Oh, Lulu," she says after tasting my sauce. "This is divine. What a beautiful job you've done. Your parents will be so proud."

"You made the lasagna, Gram," I insist. "I just helped like I always do. It's your recipe and you added the basil I forgot. You made it."

She smiles indulgently. "If you say so."

I set the timer and start to clean the kitchen. "Promise me, Gram. Promise me you won't say I made the lasagna."

Gram frowns, but nods. "If it's so important to you, my sweet girl, then I won't tell them. And you know I am proud of you, yes?"

This is one of the reasons I love her so much. No

matter what I say or do, she tries to figure me out. I hug her tight and feel the thin bones of her back beneath my hands, the aroma of tomato sauce and onions filling my nostrils. Another memory to file away.

Once the lasagna is in the oven, I leave Clay playing quietly with his trucks and Gram reading in her chair. I run up to my room, back to the mysterious black book.

I lock the door and open the book to the first page. *Click.* I memorize the pattern of symbols and try several Cyrillic keyboards on my phone. Then I try Google Translate and Bing Microsoft Translator. Both say the same thing.

I blink. My grandmother was born and raised in California. How and, more importantly, *why* does she have a book handwritten in Russian?

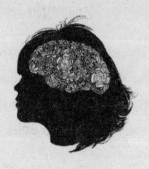

8.
Give Me a C

There is a caudate nucleus on each side of the brain. They are shaped like the letter *C* and are linked to long-term memory and things you do automatically, like read or tie your shoelaces. The brains of those with HSAM have enlarged caudate nuclei. So, basically, my brain is like a really hyper cheerleader shouting out cheers over and over. Each memory triggering another, like C-shaped dominoes.

* * *

Much to my frustration, no matter how many memories flash before me, they don't help me solve the problem of translating Russian. After spending an hour trying to understand one sentence, I close the book with a thud. The Russian Cyrillic alphabet makes it doubly hard to figure out. At this rate, translating the book will take me all summer. I even downloaded a translation app, but it skipped over words, and I started to get a headache trying to piece the broken messages together.

I need to find another way—a faster way. I shove the book under my mattress and head downstairs. Mom and Clay are watching some boring kiddie show in the family room, which means Gram is either resting or watching her own shows.

Mom gives me a sleepy smile over Clay's tousled curls. Warmth fills me to my fingers and toes, and I smile back. It's a good day when she cuddles Clay and actually sees me. It reminds me of what used to be.

Click. Shimmering squares float in front of me. Somehow I know that each one is a memory of what it was like before Maisie died. Instead of appearing in a map or calendar form, these are more like a game board marching across the room. Like a giant Candy Land game, each square a day full of memories.

It sort of makes sense—my brain must have automatically stored these memories in a way that made sense to a three-year-old. I reach out and touch one. It opens, and I hear Mom's laughter, lighter than the wind chimes outside.

Click. The first square: Mom swings me up in her arms and tickles my chin. The soft scratchiness of her nails against my skin. My own shrieks of laughter echo in the air around me.

Days line up in colorful cubes. I pick one after another.

Each memory is another version of the same joy. In every one, Mom spends hours with me. She reads to me, sings to me, brushes my hair, and plays games with me. Then Dad comes home, and we go on walks and eat together. They laugh and kiss and take turns kissing me.

This autobiographical memory of mine might not be so bad. There are lots of good memories. Proof that my family wasn't always broken. That maybe, just maybe, we can get back to the way it used to be.

I close the game board of memories and tuck it back into place. Energy pumps through me, and I hold on to the happiness still tingling in my fingers and toes. The individual memories are filed away, but the warmth and laughter still hang in the air around me.

I can't forget how Mom and Dad turned away from me. But I also can't forget all that happened before they did. Each memory—good and bad—is a part of me. Each feeling stays with me, just as clear as the day it happened.

Later that evening I knock on Gram's door. She's getting ready for bed, her hair pinned to her head in tight curls. I'm always fascinated with how different she looks without her hair done and with no makeup on. Even her long blue robe transforms her into a more relaxed version of herself.

"Night, Gram."

She holds out her arms and kisses both of my

cheeks. "Good night, my sweet girl. Is everything all right? You seem worried. The lasagna was a huge success."

Gram sees all. Even when she's not herself, she can sense when I'm struggling. I make an effort to smile. "I am a little worried about you," I admit. "You get kind of forgetful sometimes, and it . . . I don't know. I wanted Mom and Dad to think you made the lasagna all on your own because I think they're worried too."

"Oh, Lulu. It's not your job to worry about me. What can I do to help you? Do you still want my stories?" She takes my hand and squeezes my fingers.

I nod, fighting the prickle of tears behind my eyes. Love swells against my chest, each breath drawing out the stinging pain of it.

"Then have them you shall. Of course, you must keep in mind that they might bore you. I'm no Judy Blume."

I giggle. "I know that. I don't need it to be fancy."

Gram rubs her hands together. "Where shall I start, then?" She glances over at the chest in the corner.

I hold my breath. What if she decides to look for the book? How will I tell her what I've done?

She looks back in my direction and pats the edge of her bed. "We'll keep this first story short since it's your bedtime."

I wiggle against the headboard, adjusting the pillows until I'm comfortable. The scent of lavender and vanilla with a hint of hair spray floats in the air around me.

She's quiet for a moment. Then she asks, "Did I ever tell you about my friend Jacob?" She says this in a rush of words, like if she doesn't get it out fast, it might not come out at all.

"No," I say.

"We were best friends." One side of her mouth tilts up in a smile that's not quite happy or sad.

"Like me and Olivia?" *Click*. The memory of today punches me out of nowhere. Of Olivia looking anywhere but at me. Of her driving away with Piper. The memory stops there, but my imagination keeps going, and I see Piper and Olivia swimming in Piper's pool like new best friends.

She nods. "Yes, like you and Olivia. Our families were very close. Our apartments were next to each other's, and our fathers worked together."

"In San Francisco?" I ask.

She frowns at me. "It doesn't matter. Do you want to hear about Jacob or not?"

Her sharp words sting, and I sit back. I'm not used to Gram talking like that. "I want to hear," I say finally.

I can't help wondering why my question upset her. I've been told all my life that Gram grew up in San Francisco, so why do I get the feeling that isn't true? If not San Francisco, then where?

Her voice softens, losing the sharp edge of seconds ago. "Jacob was extremely smart, but he could never beat me in chess. It used to upset him whenever I won. Then one day he figured out how to distract me enough so he could beat me." She laughs and slaps her leg. "He told me I looked pretty in my blue sweater. After that he flattered me whenever he wanted to beat me at anything, the cheater. I'm still a sucker for a good compliment, yes?"

I grin. There's a lightness to her, and I can imagine her as a young girl with her blue sweater and sparkling eyes. "What did he look like?"

"Oh, he was tall and quite dashing, with dark hair and light-blue eyes. He saw everything. Nothing got past him. . . ." Her words fade along with her smile. "Poor Jacob. He was the one who needed protection, not me."

I wait for her to continue, but she's lost in her thoughts. Finally, she shakes her head and claps her hands together. "Enough for tonight, yes? I will share more tomorrow."

"Okay. Thanks, Gram." I kiss the papery skin of her cheek. "Love you."

"Love you more." Her soft reply fades behind me with the click of her door.

9.
Declarative Memory

Our declarative memory is in charge of events and facts that go into our long-term memory. It's made up of our knowledge and experiences. People used to think this kind of memory was fixed, but our memories actually change each time we speak about them. Each memory wrestles with another to be the one remembered, like a thumb war inside our brain. Little details can change every single time we revisit them. The very act of remembering can change our original memory.

* * *

I lock my door and open the Russian book gingerly. I use Google Translate and try to find Jacob's name, but the words swirl in a mess of confusion, mimicking how I feel.

Instead of answering my questions, Gram's opened up a whole wide world of new questions. Why not tell me where she lived when she and Jacob were friends? What if the book belonged to her mother and not her? Why hasn't Dad said anything to me about his mom or his grandmother knowing Russian?

I make up my mind to ask Gram the next morning. I shut the book and it slips out of my hands, bouncing lightly on the soft carpet next to my bed. When I reach down to pick it up, I notice a bulge in the back.

Was it there before?

Slowly, I pry open the back. A seam comes undone, and I tug on a piece of thick cardboard stuck inside. It slides out to reveal a small booklet with Cyrillic letters scrawled across the front. Inside there's a picture of a girl who looks just like me.

It's a Russian passport, and the girl in the picture is Gram.

I can barely breathe. I look at it closer, examining each line of her face for differences that might give an explanation. I poke the space where the passport was hidden, fishing my finger in the pocket and feeling the hard edge of another booklet. I find a pencil and use the edge to work it out.

Another passport slips free, but this one has a French seal on the cover. The picture inside is of Gram as a young woman, about the age my mom is now.

I'm sweating. I can't ask Gram any of this. Not without knowing what *this* even is. I sink to the ground and clutch the passports to my chest. The pencil I used to pry them out rolls along the floor away from me.

Dad *has* to know something about this. If I find out what he knows, then I'll know what to ask Gram without her getting upset or sad . . . or forgetting who I am.

I close my eyes. Dad told me once that Gram

used to travel for her job and that there were times she was gone for days. He said Grandpa would make hamburgers every night for dinner. To this day Dad is still sick of hamburgers.

Finding Gram's traumatic memory will be almost impossible if she won't say anything about her past. And how can I even trust that she'll tell me the truth? She's kept a book written in Russian with foreign passports hidden underneath the cover.

There is so much I don't know. I don't know what her job was or why she traveled so much. I don't know why she never told me or if my dad even knows any of this. The more I find, the more I don't know.

I need a plan.

"Dad." I smile sweetly and hand him a plate of chocolate chip cookies I've baked. "These are for you."

It's not that Dad won't spend time with me if I ask. He loves me, I know he does. But there's a chance he'll say he's busy, and this is too important to leave to chance.

He grabs two cookies and ruffles my hair. "Thanks,

sweetie. These look delicious. What's the occasion?" Suddenly his eyes widen in alarm. "Did I miss your riding competition?"

"No," I quickly say, even though he has every right to feel guilty. He's missed more than he's made. "I just wanted to make you something."

"That's very sweet of you."

"And . . ." I take a breath. This has to be delivered right or it'll be a "we'll see," which everyone knows really means no. "I was thinking about how much I miss you. We never hang out anymore, and I'm super interested in your job. I was thinking I might want to be a teacher."

"Really?" His jaw-popping smile means my compliments are working. "You know, if you really feel that way, you can come with me one day. Watch me lecture, and we can eat lunch in the cafeteria. I remember how much you loved that."

A memory sparks. *Click*. It was after Mom had Clay, and Dad had taken me to work with him for most of that summer. He and I ate ice cream while we watched students walk by. I thought then he wanted to spend time with me. I know now that he was just trying to keep me away from Mom.

What would he say if I told him that three years ago on Friday, June 24, we ate green Popsicles and he spilled coffee on his blue dress shirt? Or that the following Wednesday he forgot me in his office and drove halfway home before he remembered? I had to wait with Doug, the custodian, in the front office, and we watched a show about mining for gold in Alaska.

I pull back on the memory, tucking it away again before the rest of the calendar distracts me. I'm still learning how to navigate the maze of pictures and emotions. Sometimes I feel that I might get sucked into one and lose myself completely.

"That would be amazing," I say, refocusing on Dad. "Can I? That way I can finish my summer essay. I bet my teacher will love it."

I wonder if I've gone too far. He studies me, but then he grins and does one of his winks where half his face scrunches in a funny imitation of an actual wink. "My class is going to love you. When were you thinking?"

"Well . . . is tomorrow too soon? I would love to start working on my essay so I can just enjoy summer without worrying about it, you know?" My voice is too peppy, but I can't seem to control it.

"Tomorrow?" He considers it while he takes another bite and chews. "I don't see why not. Remember it's a summer class, so it's not as full, but there are some promising students that can really make the discussions lively."

"That sounds so fun." I dial back the bright smile when he stares at me a little too long.

"Are you okay, Lulu? Is there something else bothering you?"

"No." I shake my head and go in for a hug. Even though I try not to rely on him or Mom too much, I sink into the hug. The world seems quieter when all I can smell is his aftershave and a whiff of coffee.

He kisses the top of my head before we're interrupted by Clay's shrieks of joy. He runs as fast as his legs will carry him and barrels into Dad. "Up, up!" he shouts until Dad swings him up and tickles him.

I head off to put the second part of my plan in

motion. I can't leave Clay alone with Gram all day. I hate to admit it, even to myself, but he's safer with Mom right now. At least until I fix Gram.

I tap on Mom's studio door, nerves zipping up and down my arms. This next part depends entirely on her mood.

Mom opens the door and waves me in. "Hey, kiddo! Come see what I'm working on."

Every color in the world seems to be splattered across the canvas. It's blended in an unusual and interesting way that's unique to Mom. She can make things that shouldn't work together and turn them into paintings so beautiful, it hurts to look at them too long. "It's really pretty, Mom. I love it."

"Yeah?" Two spots of pink bloom like roses on her cheeks.

People say Mom is one of the most beautiful women in the world. Dad loves to tell the story of when they first met. How he actually couldn't speak once he saw her. But his shyness didn't stop him from writing poetry about her and leaving it at her door. She loved the poems so much, she tracked him down and asked him out. In a way he tricked her—she thought she was getting another artist, one who would understand the world she disappeared into so frequently. Instead she got a history major who ripped off his roommate's poetry trying to win her love.

Mom said it was too late once she found out. She'd already fallen for him. Dad's complete devotion to her overshadowed his lack of poetry. She was, and still is, the most important person in the world to him.

"I love all the colors," I say.

Mom beams at me and it's like sunshine. She focuses all her attention on me as if she finds me fascinating. I warn myself not to fall for it. It's how she is with anyone admiring her art.

The squares of memories beckon me. *Go back to when she loved you most*, they say. *Remember how she painted with you? How she taught you how to mix color?* I work to push the memories away, but my brain won't let me. They play out in front of me while I try to pay attention to Mom. It's weird to see her in the past and now. The contrast is like one of her paintings—colors dripping across the canvas and fading into something else entirely.

"I knew you'd get it. You have such a wonderful eye." Mom tugs me into a hug, the soft curve of her arms cushioning my cheek. When I first started preschool, I used to lean against her just like this while she practiced the alphabet with me. Learning to read is forever linked with her cool, silky skin.

I close my eyes, but it doesn't shut out the memory. Young Mom kisses me on my forehead.

I open my eyes, looking past the memory and into the present. "Mom, can I ask you something?"

Present Mom leans back, just enough to peer down at me. "Anything, Lulu."

I have to be careful. I can't just ask her to watch Clay. She'll have an excuse and then get all misty as she stares at her newest painting. Even before Maisie died, Mom was easily distracted. The artist in her longed to create. It's part of her, so how can I hate it?

"I've been missing you," I say. "Can we spend a day together, just us?"

"Oh!" Her smile hitches higher. "Maybe we can go shopping tomorrow? And then get our nails done. How does that sound?"

It sounds perfect. My heart squeezes, and I suddenly want this to be real. But it's not. It's not. It's not. It's not.

"That would be awesome," I say, and I hear the excitement in my voice. I stopped pretending sometime after her hug. "Can we talk about your art, too? I need to ask one of my parents about their job and sort of shadow them, you know?"

"You want to interview me?" She places a graceful hand over her chest as if she can hardly hold in her joy. "That would be wonderful. How long would it take?"

"All day."

Her smile slips, as I knew it would. For someone who spends all day in her studio, a whole day is too much to spend with anyone else. This is her refuge, her space that she'll share for a moment or two, but not longer than that. I'm not sure if it's because she doesn't want to, or if she really can't. I only know this is how it's been since Maisie died.

"I love that you want to know more about my work," she says with a dip in her voice. "But . . ."

"Dad says he wants me to shadow him that day." I make a face like I'm unsure, ignoring the dull pain blossoming like a flower across my rib cage. I can't seem to stop it, even though I planned this.

"Dad?" She grabs hold of the idea. "You can't hurt his feelings, Lulu. He misses you so much. I don't want to be selfish and keep you all to myself. You go with him while he teaches. Remember how much you loved it when you were little?"

"I guess." I force a smile.

Her eyes drift to the canvas.

"I guess it might be fun to go to school with Dad," I say, and her eyes snap back to me, her shoulders dropping in relief.

"Yes, that would be so good for you both."

"But what about Clay?" I say in a monotone. "Gram has lunch with her friends tomorrow. I was supposed to babysit."

Mom waves a hand. "Don't worry. I'll paint when he naps. It'll be fine."

I hug her, clinging harder than I should. "Thanks, Mom. I'll tell Dad and Gram."

She pats me absentmindedly, her attention no longer mine. I try to hold on to the feeling of success I had just a few seconds before, but it hurts even more with the contrasting memory next to it. Young Mom holding me tight and refusing to let me go.

When present Mom walks to her painting and picks up the brush, I know it's my cue to leave. I pretend to go, but I leave the door open a crack, just enough to peek into a world I'm no longer part of.

Sometimes I want to hate her for how she shuts me out, but my heart won't let me. I still want to talk to her about boys, to giggle with her like I see Olivia and her mom do.

But Gram never turns away from me. I race down the stairs, my half-formed plan spiraling in a tornado of fear. If I can't cure her, who will see me?

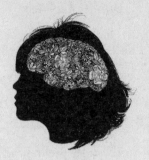

10.
Golden Gate Corpus Callosum

un fact about me: I write with my left hand and do everything else with my right. They've found that ambidextrous people—those who can use both hands—have a thicker corpus callosum, which is a bridge that helps the two parts of the brain talk to each other, like the Golden Gate Bridge connecting San Francisco to our county (Marin County).

The left side of the brain is the scientific, logical part and controls the right side of the body. The right side of the brain is in charge of creativity and controls the left side of the body. Does that mean the left side of my body is the creative part? Is that why Mom paints with her left hand?

Gram says her mother, my great-grandmother, cried the first time she saw the Golden Gate Bridge. She'd imagined it as a bridge made of solid gold shining the way to her new life in America. The dull red was a disappointment. She saw it as a sign that life isn't made of dreams. You have to make your own.

I love driving over the bridge when the fog hides it from view and all you see are the tips of its rust-colored towers. When the sun peeks through, the rust becomes a brilliant red color, better than any gold-colored bridge. It whispers to me, telling me to dream big and never give up.

I'm not sure why my great-grandmother couldn't see that. But if all she saw was a dull red bridge and she still wanted to make her own dreams come true, then I can understand why Gram loved her so much. She sounds like the kind of person who doesn't give up easily.

All my life Gram has told me her mother was from a little village in France. Dad says he loved her accent and how it made everything she said mysterious. Could the accent he remembered actually have been Russian?

"Dad?"

He sips out of his coffee cup and changes lanes after a quick glance in his side mirror. "Yeah?"

"Did your grandma ever speak French to you?"

"That's a random question," he says with a laugh. "Well, let me think. Now that you mention it, I'm not sure she ever did. Your gram was always on her case about speaking only English. By the time I was born, she'd been in this country long enough to be somewhat fluent. And you know she died when I was pretty young. I think I was seven or eight."

"Did she teach Gram any French?"

"Why so interested?" He smiles at me like he does when I amuse him.

I fiddle with my seat belt. "I was thinking I might want to learn French."

"It's a beautiful language. Gram could help you with it. I don't think you forget your first language."

I try to untangle his sentence. "Why is French Gram's first language? Wasn't her dad American?"

"Her stepdad," Dad says, and I blink in surprise. "Gram lived in France as a little girl. Her biological dad died, and my grandmother moved here for a new life."

"What? I didn't know that!" I twist and stare at him. "You always said Gram grew up in the city."

"She did, sort of. She and my grandmother moved here when Gram was a young girl."

My mind is reeling. I guess that might explain the French passport. But why the Russian one?

"Where in France did she grow up?" I ask. "Did she ever tell you about her friend Jacob?"

"I'm not sure. I think near Paris?" He glances over at me with a funny smile. "Lots of questions about Gram. I have some albums and things in the garage if you're interested. I'm not sure I remember a Jacob, though."

"I'd like that." I fidget in my seat with all the questions I want to ask. I don't want Dad to know why

I'm trying to find out about Gram's past, so I need to be careful. But if he knows about France, then maybe he'll know why she knows Russian. "Did Gram ever live in Russia?"

He frowns, and my stomach drops. Have I asked one too many questions?

"Why would you ask that? France and Russia are nowhere near each other. As far as I know, Gram's never even been to Russia, much less lived there. Matter of fact, I don't think she's even left the United States. Not since she arrived here when she was about your age."

"Oh, yeah. I was just wondering about the accent she has sometimes. Doesn't it sort of sound Russian?" I ask. I watch his expression for any sign he knows what I'm talking about.

"Yeah, your mom and I were talking about the accent thing," he says. "But I think she's just been tired lately. And now that you mention it, it might be her French upbringing coming out. When I was a little boy, sometimes she'd say things in French. I used to love that."

Dad pulls into the parking lot next to the stucco buildings of the college. A small group of kids call out a greeting to him as they walk by. He waves and grins, his shoulders higher than they are at home, his steps lighter as we walk inside the ivy-covered building.

Now all I want is to be at home so I can look through the stuff in the garage. Who knows what I might find.

Dad strides to the front of the classroom and waves me in. "Good morning, hooligans. This is my daughter, Lulu. She's here to keep you on your toes."

Fifty heads swivel in my direction. I try to ignore them as I sit in the chair Dad's saved for me. But all I can think of is how there's so much I don't know about Gram. And I thought I knew her better than anyone.

When we get home, Dad delivers on his promise and shows me the pile of boxes. Most seem to be filled with pictures of people I don't know.

I choose a box and take books and albums out

one by one to start from the bottom. After a while my neck gets all stiff like it does when I lift my saddle too high, and my eyes burn from studying every picture looking for a clue. It takes me hours just to get through one box.

I pick the albums up, ready to put them back in the box when I notice two loose pictures wedged along the bottom flap. I scoop them out. One looks like a picture of Moscow, with buildings that are like colorful Hershey's Kisses. The other is of the same girl in the passport.

First the Russian passport and now a picture of Gram in what has to be Russia. I can't ignore the evidence piling up. Dad might not know Gram lived in Russia, but I think there's a lot that she's kept from him. That she's kept from me.

What else has she kept from us?

I spend the rest of the night on Google Translate. It's painfully slow and my brain starts to throb, but I finally manage to piece together the first page of the book.

January 3, 1958. Mama gave me this journal to help

make sense of my life. She say write down what make me afraid, to take away the power from it.

Tatyana my name is, and I will to turn thirteen soon. I love books and love my cat, name Tiny Gray. He likes to sleep with me when it is cold. And always it is cold.

I look at the page. The grammar isn't perfect, but it's close enough for me to know this book is a journal. Gram's journal, from when she was my age and living in Russia.

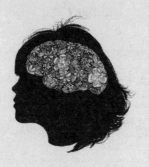

11.

The Brain Stem Is a Spy

The stem of a flower isn't the pretty part, but without it the bud would have no way to get water and food from the soil. Our brain stem is like that. It connects the brain to the spinal cord. It helps control our breathing, digestion, and blood movement. It helps the brain read the body's messages. It deciphers the complex code like a CIA agent.

Once I tell Olivia about Gram's passports and the journal, I instantly wish I hadn't. I know how much she loves a mystery, and she's been so distant lately. I thought if we solved this together, it might bring us back to the way things used to be.

"She's a spy," Olivia whispers, looking around dramatically.

"Just because she has a passport from Russia doesn't make her a spy." My voice squeaks like I've sucked helium out of a balloon.

"It's like we learned in history. The United States was practically at war with Russia. She must have moved here to spy on America. Like that TV show *The Americans*."

"I'm not allowed to watch that show."

Olivia wrinkles her nose. "I'm not either, but do you think that stopped me? This couple sounds and looks totally American, but they're really Russian spies. They have kids and everything."

"Are the kids spies?"

She frowns, like she's trying to remember. "I don't think so. I'm pretty sure they don't know a thing. Sound familiar?"

It did. My dad didn't seem to know Gram was

really from Russia. And she did have a lot of secrets. But it's *Gram*.

"That's silly. Gram's too old, and she takes care of us all the time. When would she have time to do spy stuff? Besides, we aren't at war with Russia anymore."

"Not now." Olivia rolls her eyes. "When she was young, duh. You said she used to travel a ton. Spies have to travel all the time. For missions and stuff."

I pat Remy's neck, taking comfort in his warm breath across my hand. He nuzzles me, searching for the apple I usually give him after riding. "Later, boy. You have to work for it, remember?"

"Besides," Olivia continues, leading her horse closer, "they probably retired her or something. Or whatever they do to spies who are too old to do anything."

"Who's a spy?" Max pops his head out of the tack room.

I jump, and Remy snorts and shuffles sideways at my reaction. "Shh, boy. It's okay," I murmur.

"Her grandmother," Olivia answers before I can stop her. I flinch. Next she'll be telling Piper.

Max holds a hand out to Remy and pulls a face. "Sorry, big guy. Didn't mean to startle you."

"He's fine, and Gram is *not* a spy." I work to keep calm for Remy's sake and place a soothing hand on his muzzle.

Max grins and steps back, holding his hands up as if I'm arresting him. "I'm not the one who said it."

I lead Remy out of the barn. The horses' hooves are muffled in the dirt as Olivia follows behind and chatters excitedly to Max. "Lulu found a Russian passport inside an old journal her Gram wrote as a little girl living in"—Olivia stops and lowers her voice dramatically—"Russia."

I take a deep breath like Mom does when she's trying to stop a panic attack. Remy tosses his head and nearly knocks me over. All of a sudden, I want to be as far away as possible. I long for the feeling I get when I'm riding and the wind hits my face. I forget everything when I ride. It's just me and Remy and the soft whisper of wind cleaning out my mixed-up brain.

"Have you tried googling her?" Olivia asks right before she swings herself up onto Brandy.

Max squints against the sun as he reaches forward to steady Remy while I mount up. "I'm pretty good at computers. I can look if you want."

My chest burns as I look down at him. "My gram isn't a spy."

"So you keep saying. Then why're you so mad?" He steps back when I urge Remy forward.

I head out of the paddock without answering. My brain shuffles through the massive amounts of information I've compiled the last week, about memory and diseases that can affect it. I'm no closer to finding a way to fix Gram than when I began. I urge Remy into a gallop, my body naturally falling into the rhythmic pattern of his gait. Seagull squawks mix with the low huffs of Remy's breath, and I feel my breathing slow.

"Wait up, Lulu!" Olivia giggles when she catches up. "I don't think anyone's ever left Max in their dust like that before. You should have seen his face. But seriously, you should let him see what he can find. It can't hurt, right?"

"Let's just ride, okay? I don't want to talk about this anymore."

She narrows her eyes. "Fine, but you know what they say about people who don't face their fears?"

It's times like this that I hate the rule Dad has for me about not riding alone. But I know Olivia, and she's not going to let any of this go. "No. What?"

"I'm not sure. I just like how it sounds." She shrugs and giggles again. "Race you to the fence!"

I hurry to follow, and for the first time since the parking lot, I forget about everything. I laugh as Remy picks up speed; the power of his muscles lengthens his strides until we're flying, soaring above the golden grass and compact earth, above the barn and trees.

"You always win," Olivia says with a good-natured smile. "Remy should have been a racehorse."

I laugh, a bubble of pure joy filling me. "He's the best. But Brandy's awesome too."

"I love her," Olivia agrees.

I turn Remy around, and we head back to the stables.

"Sometimes I wish I could take Brandy and ride off forever," Olivia says so softly I almost don't hear her.

I leap at the fantasy. It's one we've talked about many times. "Life on the open trail, like modern-day cowgirls."

"But I'm not sure I could live without shopping." Olivia giggles again, but this time it's forced. Is something bothering her? Is it me?

I squint in her direction, trying to figure out her mood. "You wouldn't need the distraction. It would be just us and the horses. Sounds pretty perfect to me."

"Sure does." But she doesn't sound convinced.

I almost tell Olivia about my memory. It would be such a relief to be able to trust her that much. I waver for a second, considering it. But I can't get Piper out of my head.

"Race you to the barn," I yell instead.

"You're on!" Olivia's reply escapes in the breeze whipping around us. She kicks Brandy into a gallop and leaves me in her dust.

I urge Remy on, and with hardly any effort, he easily catches up. We gallop beside Brandy and Olivia at an easy pace, but I pull him back at the very end. Olivia cheers as she beats me to the barn, and

I'm about to smile until I look past her to see Max watching me.

Grit settles in my mouth with a tinge of embarrassment. Does he know I let Olivia win?

This is something I'm not sure how to handle. Olivia and I've been friends since the first grade. I want to believe that she wouldn't drop me even if she knew the whole truth about my memory. But I'm afraid that she might, so I find myself doing things like letting her win.

Olivia laughs and hugs me when I get off Remy. "Sorry, Lulu. Is it wrong that I'm super excited to finally beat you in a race?"

"It's about time," Max says with his usual smirk turned up even more obnoxiously than usual. "Remy looks mad at you, Lulu. Did you throw the race or something?"

Max raises one brow like he's waiting for me to confess. He might be guessing, but I'm pretty sure he knows. My palms start to sweat.

I narrow my eyes, trying to signal what I'll do to him if he even thinks about telling Olivia. He just grins and starts unbuckling Remy's saddle.

Olivia's smile slips as she reads her texts. "I have to run. Can you take care of Brandy for me?"

"Sure." I grab Brandy's reins, and Olivia stalks off, her boots kicking at the dirt.

"Emergency?" Max asks, taking Brandy from me.

I grab a brush and start on Remy's back. "I guess."

He spins the cap on his head, and it makes the top part of his hair stick out. I wait for him to ask why I let Olivia win, but he surprises me by saying, "Did you want me to see what I can find out about your grandma? I know you guys are close, so I get why you want to know what's up."

I'm about to answer when Clay's excited shouts grab my attention. Gram's van is pulled up by the barn, and Clay is holding his stuffed elephant out the window. Gram waves me forward. "Hurry, Lulu, I'm late."

"Go ahead," Max says. "I'll finish this."

"Thanks." I turn to leave and then pause. "Can you double-check where she was born?" I ask in a rush. "Like, if I can give you a country or some place to search?"

He holds out his hand. "Give me your phone."

I give it to him, and he punches in his number. His phone vibrates, and he waves it at me. "Text me all the info you have."

I shove my phone back in my coat and run to Gram.

"Hey, what are you late for?" I ask her. I know her schedule as well as my own, and there are no appointments that I'm aware of. I'm usually the one who keeps track of that for her.

"It's with my friend who's a doctor. Remember the one I told you about?"

"Yeah." I try not to sound skeptical.

Gram hands Clay a cracker while I toss my riding gear in the trunk. "Yakov said I could meet him at his office in ten minutes. He's squeezing me in."

"Yakov? What kind of name is that?"

She's quiet for a second before she turns on the van. "Just a name," she says, her voice quivering.

I swallow past the lump in my throat.

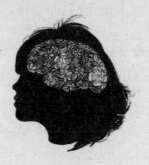

12.

Frontal Lobe

There are lobes in the brain that are super important. They aren't like earlobes, with no purpose other than to dangle jewelry. The frontal lobe makes something called dopamine, which helps nerve cells in the brain talk with one another. We use this part of the brain to make plans.

What was Gram's plan?

The doctor's visit lasted all of ten minutes. Gram is back in the car before Clay finishes his juice box.

It's barely given me time to text Olivia to see why she had to leave so quickly.

"That was fast."

"I'm as healthy as a horse," Gram says with a brilliant smile. "Yakov took one look at me and gave me a clean bill of health. He promised to call your dad tomorrow with the results."

"He didn't need to do any tests?" I know I sound suspicious, but I can't help myself. I *am* suspicious.

"He did, and I passed with flying colors." She drives home slower than usual, her fingers tapping to a beat only she hears.

We pull into the driveway, and Gram puts the van in park. She frowns and tugs on the key still in the ignition. When it doesn't come out, her hands shake and she sits back in her seat. Her eyes close with a flutter.

"It's okay," I murmur. I pull out the key for her and open the back door so I can grab Clay. "I'll get Clay. Do you want to go inside and ask Mom for a cup of tea?"

"Yes, thank you, sweet girl. I'm feeling very tired, I think."

"Tired" has become the code word for forgetful or confused.

I hand Clay off to Mom and make Gram a cup of tea. She settles in front of the television and falls asleep.

Mom sniffs Clay's hair. "When's the last time you had a bath, big boy?" She glances at me with raised brows. "Has Gram washed his hair lately?"

I bristle. How dare she act like this is Gram's fault? Gram isn't his mother. "I think so," I bite out.

"Let's go scrub-a-dub-dub you," Mom sings, propping Clay on her hip. She gives me a quick smile, but it doesn't reach her eyes. They look mad.

I close my eyes and play back the last week. My memory screeches with hundreds of seconds of rewinding as I search for a time Gram might have given Clay a bath. The last time was nearly eight days ago. No wonder he stinks.

A peach pit of worry shoves against my ribs. The brochure to the retirement home is torn into bits and thrown away in the trash can outside, and I haven't seen or heard anything more about sending Gram away. But that doesn't mean Mom and Dad won't start thinking about it again.

I add Clay's bath time to the growing list of things I need to double-check for Gram. As I think about everything I need to keep track of, I feel a weight settling on me, like when I have to hoist Remy's saddle on his back. It takes all my strength, and my arms shake so hard, sometimes I'm afraid I'll drop it.

As soon as I can, I lock myself in my bedroom. Piled in the corner are the heaps of albums I've been going through. Most of them show Dad as a baby, with Gram and Grandpa Daniel smiling and laughing in all the pictures.

Grandpa Daniel died before I was born, but I can tell I would have liked him. His eyes are smiley all the time, even when he's looking straight-faced at the camera.

I take the passport out of the book I hid it in. Tatyana Petrov. I text the name to Max.

I change out of my riding clothes and grab some of the albums. I need to at least try to talk to her. I don't want to make her emotional and cause a "tired" episode, but I can't help thinking about Olivia's idea of Gram being a spy. I need to find out more about Gram's past. Even if that means I risk making Gram mad at me.

The aroma of dinner leads me to the kitchen. Gram flashes me a smile and hands me a knife. "Just in time to chop the celery."

I pick up the celery and place it on the cutting board. "Gram, can I hear more about your friend Jacob?"

I start chopping while she stirs the meat she's browning. "Ah, Jacob. Last time I told you about our chess games, yes?"

I smile. Her remembering was a good sign. "Yes, Gram. You said you used to always beat him at chess."

She snorts in a very un-Gram-like fashion. "Unless he cheated. One time when we were playing, I beat him and he tried to convince me he was the one who should have won." Her laugh fades along with her smile.

I stop chopping and lean closer.

"That's the afternoon his papa came home early."

She pauses, still stirring the meat. Her mouth takes on a thin, grim line. I almost tell her she doesn't need to go on, but before I can say anything, her voice changes, going up like she's out of breath.

It's the voice of a little girl.

"Jacob's papa could be most charming, but there were also times when he was very scary, yes?" Her accent gets thicker as she continues. "That night Jacob's papa flung the front door open so hard, it hit the wall. Pictures fell off and broke. He sounded like a monster on a rampage. Jacob and I hid in the closet, and he held my hand tight until the yelling and crying stopped. He told me his papa turned into another person when he had too much vodka. I thought I'd be happy when I could no longer hear his papa yelling . . . but the silence was almost worse.

"When his mama came to let us out of the closet, one of her eyes was black and sealed shut. She told me to go home, but I didn't want to leave Jacob there. He told me they would be all right, that his papa had passed out and he wouldn't wake up again until morning. When I got home, my mama hugged me tight. She sang to me until I fell asleep. I wished she could have done the same for Jacob."

Gram slowly opens her eyes. She smiles at me. "Will you tell your dad and mom that dinner is almost ready?"

My heart beats as fast as a hummingbird's wings. How can she look so normal after telling me such a terrible story?

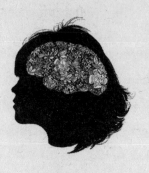

13.

Skull

Our skulls safeguard our brains from the outside world. But sometimes, like in a car accident, the very thing that's supposed to protect the brain actually injures it. The force of the accident can cause the brain to slam against the bones of the skull, causing a concussion. The effects of a traumatic brain injury can cause long-term damage.

I think of this, and I think of how parents are supposed to protect their children. I think of Gram's friend Jacob and how he must have felt all those years ago when the person who was supposed to protect him hurt him instead.

I'm on my way to tell my parents that dinner is ready when my phone buzzes.

Olivia: I'm sorry I had to leave without helping with the horses

Olivia: Did you ask your gram about

Olivia: the passports and the journal??

Me: Not yet. She just told me a really sad story and I found a picture of her in Russia when she was like our age. I don't know what to do. Should I ask her?

Olivia: NOOOO!! What if she's

Olivia: a spy??????

Olivia: She might have to tell the government

Olivia: that you know. You could put her and your family

Olivia: in danger!!!!!

I roll my eyes. Did I really think I would get advice instead of her wild theories?

Me: She's not a spy!!!!! Ugh, Olivia. Just stop with that stuff.

Olivia: Fine, but you should listen to me. Did you hear back from Max yet?

Me: Not yet.

Olivia: Do you need me to come over? I can have my mom drop me off. I could spend the night

Me: Let me ask my dad

I find Dad in his office. "Gram says it's time for dinner."

Dad looks up from his desk, which is covered with papers. He has the faraway look he gets when he's grading homework. "Thanks, hon. Can you ask her to bring me a plate?"

"Can Olivia spend the night?"

He nods, not really hearing me. "Sure, okay."

"Can we go to the park?"

He nods again. "Yeah, sounds good."

A good thing about a distracted dad is he always says yes to everything.

Mom's lips pinch shut when I say Dad wants to eat in his office. She takes a quick taste of the spaghetti while she makes him a plate. Her hand flies to cover her mouth. "How long did you cook the pasta, Sue?"

My stomach jumps to my throat and then free-falls to my toes. I know before I take a bite that the spaghetti noodles aren't right.

I take a forkful and nearly chip my tooth. Gram didn't cook it long enough. I forgot to double-check and set the timer for her.

"Sorry, Gram," I rush to say. "I forgot to set the timer like you asked me to. I was texting with Olivia and got distracted. I must have poured it in the strainer too soon."

Gram blinks in confusion. "You did?"

Mom puts another pot of water on to boil. "We'll just make some more. Your sauce is delicious as usual, Sue. Don't worry, Lulu. You're still learning. I remember when I first started to cook. I nearly burned the kitchen down."

My cheeks tremble when I smile. Taking the fall for Gram is worth Mom thinking I can't even set a timer right. If it means Gram stays with us, then I'll take the blame for every last thing.

Olivia's mom drops her off just as we're finishing dinner. "Hi, all," Olivia says with a wave. She sticks her tongue out at Clay and he giggles.

"Hello, dear," Mom says. "Love the bracelets."

Olivia lifts her arm and shakes the silver bangles. "Thanks, Mrs. C."

"Dad said we could go to the park," I tell Mom.

She looks over in surprise and glances at Gram. "Um, I guess that sounds okay. What do you think, Sue?"

Gram hands Clay his juice before glancing over at me. "You girls didn't get your fill of each other today?"

I push my chair out. "Olivia has something she needs to talk to me about. It's personal stuff."

Olivia shuffles nervously and manages to look suitably pathetic.

"As long as you follow the rule to be back before dark," Gram says. "Does that sound reasonable, Rose?"

Mom nods and smiles at Olivia. "How are your mom and dad? I haven't spoken to Felicity in weeks."

Olivia's eyes dart from Mom to me like she doesn't know what to say. I stare back at her with a faint frown. Olivia always knows what to say. "She's busy with . . . um . . . her job."

"We'll be back before dark," I say, linking arms with Olivia and tugging her out of the kitchen.

We're halfway down the driveway when I whisper, "Thanks for coming."

"Well, you needed me, so . . ."

I smile. "So, about your personal stuff."

Her giggle is the same from earlier today. The forced laugh, the one that stretches her mouth too wide. "Funny. Now, tell me why we're going to the park. Don't you have piles of photo albums you still need to look at? I can help."

"I told Max to meet us there."

She tugs me to a stop. "What! Did he find something about your gram?"

I start walking again. "He said he found something, and I didn't want him to bring it to the house."

"I knew it! He found out she's a spy," Olivia says. She hurries past me and opens the small metal gate designed to keep little kids from escaping.

Max is perched on the edge of a swing. A couple

of swings down from him, a mother is trying to get her toddler out. When the boy throws a tantrum, Max hops up to help untangle the child's legs.

"There you go, buddy," he says. The boy stares up at him with fascination. The boy's mom thanks him. Who knew that Max Rodriguez was such a softy?

Max's smile kicks up to a grin when he glances over and sees us. "Hey!"

"You find out her gram's a spy?" Olivia sits on one of the swings and pushes off with her foot.

"Stop calling her that," I say automatically, my eyes going to the paper in his hands.

Max hands it to me and runs a hand through his hair. He nods to the benches near the slide. "Sit and read. We can talk after."

Olivia jumps off the swing and plops next to me on the bench. She tries to read the paper over my shoulder. "What does it say?"

Brains use chemicals and electricity to either find memories or store them for later. Mine, as I read, is exploring data it's already collected. It can determine in advance if there's a point to the search. The hippocampus and frontal cortex analyze a variety of things to decide if they're worth remembering. Other brains, without HSAM, might discard a memory that doesn't seem important. But my brain holds on to it. I hoard the memories in a hidden maze of cells, lobes, and intricate pathways too detailed for me to fully understand, no matter how hard I try.

"It says Tatyana Petrov was born in Moscow, Russia," I say. "Her father was a politician, and her mother was a professional ballerina before she gave birth to Tatyana. When she was thirteen, Tatyana and her mother disappeared. No one knows what happened to them."

Max shoves both hands in his pockets and leans against the slide. "I ran the name through immigration records here, but there wasn't anyone with that name. Then I tried to find out more about her life in Russia, but there was nothing else. The only reason I found out this much was because her father was a pretty big-deal politician and he put out a reward for information about them."

I shake my head. "None of this makes sense."

"I did some reading," Max says. "I guess it was really hard for people to just leave Russia. If someone left, it was usually kept secret because it embarrassed the government or something. Maybe this dude, the dad, managed to smuggle his wife and daughter out to America, to get them somewhere safe. Then he says they've disappeared. Boom. They're safe and he's not in trouble."

"Why wouldn't he go with them?" Olivia asks, her face pale. "I mean, a dad should stay with his family, right?"

"If he was an important politician, maybe he couldn't leave as easily as they could," I say. "But why is there no record of them here?"

"No record of a Tatyana Petrov that matches your gram's age. But there is a Susan Smith and her mother, Mary. They arrived in San Francisco on May 2, 1958, from Paris, France. I tried looking for immigration records from France, but so far there's nothing."

"They changed their names." I close my eyes, the information like a computer code scrolling across my eyelids. "To protect them from something?"

"Maybe," Max agrees. "Or . . . the Russian government could have sent them to the United States as spies."

I grit my teeth. "Why do you both think that my gram is a spy? You've met her. Does she seem like a spy to you?"

"Which is what would make her a good one," he insists. "A good spy can fit in anywhere. They're adaptable, smart, good with language. Can you think about any time she did something that seemed the slightest bit suspicious?"

Olivia kicks at the wood chips on the ground around us and stares at me with wide eyes. "You have to remember something."

I pull off my shoe to shake out the wood chips lodged in the heel. The dust from the wood floats in the air and fills it with the scent of freshly cut trees. The smell triggers a faded memory peeking around the crisp edges of now. *Click.*

Gram is arguing with a man while I gather sticks. I'm five. It's March 2, 2011, on a Wednesday, and Gram is babysitting me while Mom and Dad are on vacation.

We're in the woods, and I want to keep exploring under logs for lizards, but she's told me to keep quiet while she talks to the strange man. I strain to hear, but they're not saying real words. The man yells at her, and she runs to me and grabs my hand. We run away, and I'm scared because I've never seen Gram cry before.

"Lulu!" Olivia's voice breaks through my thoughts, and I look up, remnants of the woods still before me. "Where were you just now?"

I brush a hand over the papers in my lap. "What does the word '*izmennik*' mean?"

"What?" Olivia's brow crinkles before her gaze flies to Max.

"It sounds Russian," he says, typing the word into his phone. "Says here it means 'traitor.'"

They both wait for me to explain. But all I can hear is the angry man shouting that Gram is a traitor as we run away.

14.

Basal Ganglia

Neurons are nerve cells that help the brain communicate with the body. There's a group of neurons that are hidden deep in the brain called the basal ganglia. Gram puts *basil* in her spaghetti sauce, and Dad says my legs are *gangly*, so I imagine this part of my brain as spaghetti noodles clustered together, helping me figure out how to move my feet and hands after I'm hit with the memory of this man shouting at Gram.

* * *

"When I was five," I say, glancing up at Max, "I remember Gram meeting with a man. He kept shouting '*izmennik*' to her. We were in the woods, and I remember running and Gram crying."

"Holy crap," Olivia mutters. "You were on a mission with her!"

"It was probably a meeting with her handler," Max says.

"What's a handler?" Olivia asks, starry-eyed. She looks at him like he knows everything.

He keeps his gaze on me. "A handler is the person who makes sure the spy is doing their job and tells them what the next one is. It's important to help keep the deep undercover agents from forgetting their jobs."

Suddenly, Gram being a spy doesn't seem so farfetched anymore. Could Max and Olivia really be right? And if that Russian man in my memory really is Gram's handler, what will he do if he finds out she's losing her memory?

"What do they do if agents stop wanting to, you know, spy?" My thoughts are spiraling, and I can barely keep up.

"Silence them forever." Olivia slices a finger across her throat. "That's what happens in movies."

The panic I'm feeling must be written all over my face because Max frowns at Olivia. "Don't worry about that right now," he says in the same gentle voice he uses with the horses. "Can you remember what woods you were in when the man chased you?"

I close my eyes and freeze the picture of Gram and me running. I examine the trees and look for something I recognize. There's a small sign near a bubbling creek.

My eyes fly open. "Samuel P. Taylor Park. We were by the creek."

"Okay," Max says with a quick laugh. "That was fast. Are you sure?"

Olivia snorts. "If she says so, then it's true. Her memory is amazing."

My stomach clenches at her words. She doesn't have any idea how "amazing" my memory really is, that I could tell them what I had for breakfast the day the Russian stranger yelled at us, or that we went to the nursery and bought seeds for Gram's garden. How would they look at me then?

"We should go," Max says. "See if the place triggers more memories. Maybe you know more than you think?"

"Ooh! Yes, Lulu. We have to go." Olivia jumps up and down, clapping her hands.

Could the actual place trigger more specific memories? Even if I can recall the memories right now, I have no way of explaining how I'm remembering. Either I tell Olivia and Max the truth or go along for a field trip.

"How will we get there?" I ask. "I don't think the bus goes out that far."

"Uber," Max says like it's no big deal. "I take it all the time. I can have a driver here in five minutes."

Olivia's eyes widen. "You can do that? I thought you had to be, like, an adult or something."

Max shrugs. "If they ask, I just tell them I'm eighteen. My dad got me prepaid Visa cards and I use them. No problem."

I shake my head. "That's lying."

He pulls his phone out, his smirk more know-it-all than ever. "And you don't lie, Lulu?"

Max calls me out with the challenge in his eyes. He knows that I pulled Remy back and let Olivia's horse win and that I'm prying into my gram's past without her knowing. Lately I've been walking a minefield of half-truths and misdirections. It's impossible for him to know all the details, but it kind of feels like he does.

"Please, Lulu. You've come this far. Don't you want to know?" Olivia clasps her hands together, begging.

I sigh. "Okay, but if the driver looks sketchy, I'm not getting in."

I can only imagine the trouble I'll be in if Gram or my parents ever find out about this, not that I'm planning on telling them.

A silver Prius pulls up with an older woman at the wheel, looking like she'd rather be doing anything else but this. At least she doesn't look a killer who will dump our bodies in the bay. So there's that.

Max sits in the front, and Olivia and I pile in

the back. I stare out the window as we head past the town of Fairfax and over the hill to the valley. Traffic is heavy, and I wonder how long it'll be before Gram gets worried. Mom and Dad might not notice at all.

Olivia chatters nonstop. Redwood trees stretch to the sky, blocking out the sun, and the darkness matches my mood. I wish I could go back to thinking my gram was nothing but a grandmother who makes the best pies. I'm afraid of what else I'll find out.

"I think we're close," Max tells the Uber driver.

"Two more miles," I say.

His gaze meets mine in the rearview mirror before turning back to the road. "That's specific."

"Yeah, really specific," Olivia agrees. "My phone isn't working out here. Is yours, Lulu?"

I keep quiet. Let them think I've looked it up on my phone. They don't need to know about the map floating in the air to the right of me. Besides, lots of people remember things from seven or eight years ago.

Olivia takes advantage of my silence to volley questions at Max about how he knows so much on the subject of espionage. Apparently, Max likes spy novels and movies. I'm taking the word of someone whose only authority is his library card.

"Here we are," the driver says. We slow down at the empty information booth, and we drive past, even though it clearly states to put the required money in the box.

"Shouldn't we pay?" I ask, unable to stop myself.

"Not if we're only going to be here a few minutes," Max answers.

The driver parks near the creek, and Max pulls open my car door.

"We should still pay," I mumble.

The scent of the trees instantly triggers the exact memory I had at the park. This time I hear what Gram is saying to me. *Don't worry, Lulu. He isn't going to hurt you. I won't ever let anyone hurt you.*

"You've got that look again," Max says. "You remembering something?"

I blink him into focus. "Maybe. I'm not sure."

He rubs a quick hand over his head and flings his arm to point out the campground. "Walk around and see if anything else pops up. Maybe you'll remember something more specific."

"Watch out for poison oak," Olivia warns. "Last time I camped, I accidentally touched some, and it was so itchy. So, like, stay on the path and don't pick up random sticks."

I nod to let her know I'm listening while I look around for something familiar. Is it weird to recognize a tree in a park you haven't been to in eight years? I recognize the nearest one, its trunk twisting in a spiral, several branches dipping low over the water.

There'd been a squirrel running between the water and me. I was trying to coax it to me while Gram talked to the man. I squeeze my eyes shut and concentrate on the words they were saying. Each word slows down, the Cyrillic alphabet punching holes in my memory of then and now.

I repeat the words out loud, the foreign sounds thick on my tongue. When I open my eyes, Olivia is staring at me with her mouth wide open. Max smiles at me while he furiously types on his phone.

"We can translate it later," he says. "But it sure sounds like Russian."

Fatigue settles in my muscles like a million pounds. "I need to get home."

Max finishes typing, and we all pile back in the car. Max asks the driver to stop at the guard gate. He hops out and stuffs a five-dollar bill in the box. His mouth isn't twisted in its usual smirk, and he meets my eyes only for a second before he looks away.

Most people who don't have artists for moms don't know how many browns there are. There is angry brown, mean brown, boring brown, sarcastic brown, gentle brown, funny brown. I used to think his eyes were sarcastic brown, but I was wrong. His eyes are a funny brown, a gentle brown. The kind horses have. The kind you can trust.

I'd rather think about Max's eyes than the very real possibility that Gram is not only a liar and a spy, but also someone else I've never really known. What do I do if that's true? Do I help her remember something that should stay forgotten?

15.

Snap, Crackle, Pop

Synapses are just what they sound like—sizzle and snap. Snap, crackle, pop goes the brain. If the nerve signals are like electricity, then the neurons are like wires. Which would make synapses the outlets we plug our lamps into. Without the snap of the synapses, there's no way for the nerve cells to turn on and talk to one another.

My synapses snap, and an electric current of information hums through me.

"Thanks for helping me," I say as the car pulls along the curb.

"I'll text you what I find." Max twists in his seat so he can look me in the eyes. He almost seems worried about me, but I push that out of my mind. It's one thing for him to not act like a jerk, but it's a whole other thing to actually be a friend.

Olivia stays in the car as I climb out. "Call me and tell me everything," she says, grabbing my hand.

"I thought you were spending the night?" I ask.

"My mom texted and she wants me to come home." Her smile is wide, but her eyes are shiny. Like she's trying not to cry.

"Is your mom okay?"

Olivia makes a face. "She's just being needy. You know how moms are."

I smile, but something twists in my stomach. I wish my mom needed me like Olivia's needs her. I want nothing more than to find Gram and hug her tight. I wave as they back out of the driveway, my fingers so numb I can barely feel them.

Gram leans against the kitchen counter with her

arms folded across her chest. "It's dark, Lulu. What's my rule?"

I walk to her, and she automatically opens her arms to hug me. I bury my face against the silky texture of her blouse. The scent of vanilla and lavender smells like home.

"Are you okay? Did something happen?"

I shake my head. "I don't feel good," I say. Another lie in the pile of lies building around me.

She examines me. Her fingers are cool against my forehead. "You don't feel warm. Why don't you go rest on the couch, and I'll make you some hot chocolate?"

My smile is wobbly at best. "Okay."

I curl up in the corner with my favorite blanket. Gram comes in once the hot chocolate is ready and hands it to me. "I know what might make you feel better. Would you like another story?"

Not after her last story. I don't want to think about anyone's dad hurting his family. Maybe Gram was right and some things should stay forgotten. Then again, how will I find what might cure Gram if I don't listen?

"Okay."

She leans back, and I place my head on her shoulder. Her voice vibrates against my cheek as she speaks.

"One winter day Jacob and I snuck out of school. We spent the day at the park near our apartment building. There was a lake in the park that had frozen over, and the ice seemed to go for miles. He dared me to walk out on it with him.

"I worried it might break and swallow us whole. I remember thinking, will the water welcome me, or spit me back out? It was so cold that ice crystals formed on our eyelashes and I could no longer feel my fingers or toes. We finally went to my apartment. My parents were at work, and we pretended it was just the two of us in the whole world, with the teakettle whistling and my cat begging us to pet him.

"I was anxious that his papa would be angry if he found out that Jacob skipped school. But Jacob told me that his papa wouldn't care. His smile seemed so carefree, but Jacob could never lie without smiling. I liked that about him. How I could tell what he was thinking or feeling even if his words said something different.

"I was furious at his papa for hurting him. Mama said some men changed when they drank too much. The alcohol changed them to someone else entirely. They could be a person you loved and then switch to someone you didn't even recognize.

"I wished Jacob had a papa like mine. That night Papa came home early and took Mama and me to the theater. We got the best seats because of Papa. His job made him very important, and people always gave him gifts. And the play was too magical to put into words. The lead actress sang like an angel."

Gram smiles dreamily, as if she could still hear the actress. She and I sit for what seems like hours after she finishes her story. She breathes like she's just done the hundred-yard dash.

"Are you okay, Gram?" I finally whisper. I sit up to meet her gaze.

The lines around her eyes droop like the fringe on the throw pillows. "Yes, my sweet girl. How are you feeling?"

"I'm better. I think I'll go to bed now."

She smiles. "Go on up and I'll come tuck you in."

I climb into bed and read until my eyes burn. After an hour, I finally give up on her coming. It's one of the first times she hasn't tucked me in when she said she would. Was it the story? Is telling her memories making things worse instead of better?

Before I go to sleep, I look up articles about Russia in the fifties. The former Soviet Union sounds like something straight out of *The Hunger Games*. Leaving the country wasn't allowed—you couldn't just buy a plane ticket. You needed special permission and a bunch of paperwork. So how did Gram and her mom escape? Were they planted here as spies? And if they were . . . what happens if the United States finds that out?

I give up on sleeping, but I must drop off at some point. Dad shakes me awake as I'm dreaming about razor wires and machine guns chasing Gram and me as we run.

"Hey, sweetie," he says. "Did you want to come in to work with me today?"

I blink and try to slow down the frantic beat of my heart.

"Um, I think I have plans with Olivia today," I say. It's kind of sweet that he wants me to come to school with him again, but there's too much at stake for me to take any time off. "Maybe next week?"

"Sure thing. Gram says you weren't feeling well last night?"

"Yeah, I'm better now." I smile to prove it.

He ruffles my hair. "Glad to hear it. See you tonight."

"Dad?"

He pauses at my door and flashes me one of his goofy smiles. "Yeah?"

I struggle with what I want to ask, so I change my mind. "I love you," I say instead.

He grins, and I'm happy I didn't ask him if he thought his mom was a Russian spy. "Love you too, Lulu Lemon."

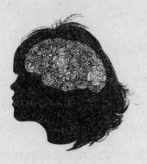

16.

Flashbulb Memory

There are memories called flashbulb memories. They are extremely intense, highly detailed snapshots of a moment that is usually very emotional to us. Like when my parents talk in hushed tones about the terrorist attacks on 9/11 like they happened yesterday instead of seventeen years ago.

These intense memories are often imprecise. We allow details of others' stories to mix with our own memories. Until we are actually remembering someone else's experience like it's our own.

* * *

Max: I translated the Russian you remembered. It means: You are a traitor. It won't matter where you hide. It will find you.

I don't tell him that I already translated it. Then I'd have to explain how remembering the Russian was as easy as closing my eyes and listening to my memory. How I could slow down what the man yelled until I heard the words one at a time. My translation was close to his with only small differences: *You betrayed me. You can't hide from it. It will always find you.*

I text back.

Me: Yeah. That doesn't sound scary or anything.

Max: It doesn't sound good.

Me: I think I'm going to just ask her if she's from Russia. I'm going to show her the journal and not tell her I found the passports. See what she says.

Max: Dude. Not sure that's a good idea, but you do what you got to. Do you want me to come over so you're not alone with her?

Me: Nah. She's my grandmother.

Max: Still a hard thing to do

Me: I'm fine. I'll let you know what happens.

Max: Wait! I don't want to tell you over the phone, but I sort of did some more digging and I found something weird. Can you come to the stables? See what it is first and then talk to her, if you still think you should. I'm working today. You can say you have a lesson. Like in half an hour?

Me: Can't you just tell me?

Max: No. I need to show you. It's important.

Me: Okay.

I text Olivia with the plan and tear my bedroom apart searching for my blue top. Olivia still hasn't responded after I finish getting ready. It isn't like her to ignore a text. She hates leaving any notifications unanswered.

I head down to the kitchen, where Mom is feeding Clay. He pours orange juice in his eggs and stirs them with a plastic dinosaur.

"Hey, Lulu. I didn't know you had a lesson today." Mom motions to my riding outfit. "Gram ran to the store, and you know I hate to go out on a Saturday."

Or any other day. I try to hide my impatience, but she sees something that gives me away. Her smile falters, and her wrist flicks as if she's painting. "Can you ask Olivia's mom to pick you up?"

I glance at my phone, but there's still no text from Olivia. "Sure, I can ask."

I text Max instead, my fingers flying.

Me: No way to get there right now.

My phone immediately buzzes.

Max: Sending an Uber.

My lies tumble from me even more effortlessly than before. "Her mom says she will."

"Great!" Mom's overly chipper voice hurts my ears. "I'm sorry I can't take you. I'm feeling stronger lately, so I thought I'd start driving you to lessons during the week. Would you like that?"

I don't know how to answer. I guess it would be okay if it were just because she wanted to spend time with me. But what if this is about her and Dad shipping Gram off to a home?

"Olivia's mom will be here in five minutes. I'll just meet her down the road so she doesn't have to back up." I grab a granola bar and duck out the door before Mom can say anything else.

I don't give her time to ask when I'll be home or any of the other hundreds of questions Gram would ask. In this instance, it works in my favor. I hurry down the road just in time to see the same Uber driver pull over.

"Hey again," she says with a friendly smile.

"Thanks for getting me."

"It's my job. Where are your friends?"

Even the Uber driver pays more attention to me. I look out the window. "I'm meeting up with them," I say. I spend the ride twisting my fingers and seeing how far they can bend.

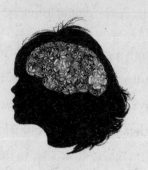

17.
Sensory Stage

We store memories in three different ways: first in the sensory stage, then in short-term, and then in long-term for those memories that stand out. Before a memory makes it to the big time, it has to get past the other two. It's kind of like our memories are auditioning for a bigger role on the stage of our lives. Will they be famous and remembered for all time, or will they be one of those actors no one knows and instantly forgets? To remember something, first we see, smell, touch, or hear something, and it triggers an emotion. The emotion, especially if it's strong enough, then pulls up the stored memory.

I *see* Max smile at me. The stables are filled with the *smell* of hay and manure. His *voice* is kind of rumbly, but it cracks and goes higher when he's excited about something. He reaches over and hands me an envelope, and his hand *brushes* mine. Sensory memory leaps right past short-term and straight to long-term memory. The moment I stopped thinking of Max as a jerk.

"Open it." He glances at the envelope I clutch in my hands.

I fold the gold-colored metal clips back so they can fit through the holes, and I take my time sliding the papers out. They slip out, inch by inch, until they're in my lap.

I glance down and then look up so fast my neck cracks. "What?"

"I know!" he says, his voice sliding up and down like a violin. "This is a file I found on your gram. It's all crossed out."

"But—but what does it mean?" I scour the pages for any words that aren't completely blotted out with thick black lines. I hold the paper up to the light, but there's no way to see what's written underneath.

"I think you know."

A knot sits in my stomach, and I press down on it. "Where did you find this?"

Max kicks at a rock. "I hacked the FBI database. Well, technically I hacked my uncle's computer. But since he works there, he has access to records the public recorder doesn't. I kept hitting a wall with how your gram immigrated here. So I offered to walk Molly—that's his beagle." He spreads his arms wide. "Then presto. While he played video games, I downloaded everything I could about your gram."

"A hacker?" I whisper. "What if you get caught?"

Max shrugs. "I won't. I'm good at it. I'm like a computer ninja."

"And so humble and shy about it."

"Hey," Max says with a smug grin. "No reason to be humble when you're the best, and I'm the best. No one will even know. And who are we hurting? No one, that's who."

I stare back down at the paper. "But why is it all crossed out like this?"

"This is what they call 'redacted.' It's when the government blacks out things they don't want anyone to know."

"Is this something else you learned from watching eighties spy movies?" I ask.

He shakes his head like I've disappointed him. "Dude, that hurts. My knowledge is so much more than movies and books. I listen when my uncle talks about his job. I know things. A lot of very important things. Plus, I'm sort of a genius. Not to brag or anything."

"Okay, I get it." I fold the paper in half. "Whatever it is must have happened a long time ago. Do you think they still care?" If Olivia were here, this is when she'd roll her eyes and say, *Duh, Lulu.*

Instead, Max looks at me patiently and speaks very slowly. "They redacted a five-page file. They obviously still care."

I fumble with my phone, but there's still no answer from Olivia. "Where is she?"

"Who?" He waves to some girls walking by, and they giggle.

"Olivia. She needs to hear this."

He ducks his head, his hair flopping over his eyes. "You haven't talked to her?"

I slip the papers back into the envelope. "Not since last night. Why?"

He won't meet my gaze. "Maybe you should call her."

My stomach lurches like I've eaten too many gummy worms. "Tell me."

He glances around to make sure we won't be overheard. "When we got to her house last night, her mom and dad were fighting. I think maybe Olivia's mom was kicking him out."

"What? But they're super in love!" Olivia always talked about all the flowers and candy her dad brought her mom. My dad only buys Mom stuff on their anniversary.

"Didn't look that way." Max tugs the bill of his

baseball cap down low. "She looked pretty upset. I didn't want to make it worse, so I left."

Was this why she didn't spend the night? All her forced smiles start to make sense. I was so worried about my problems that I'd completely missed hers. I nearly drop my phone as I pull up her number. "I need to call her."

Max grabs a shovel and nods to the stalls next to us. "I need to clean these. I'll call you later, okay?"

"Yeah," I say as I head back down the road. I wait until I have better cell service before I call.

Olivia immediately picks up. "Lulu?"

"Hey, you okay?"

Her voice quivers so much I can barely make out the words. "My dad left."

"What?" I don't know what the right thing to say is. I press the phone harder against my cheek.

"They've been fighting, and last night—" She's crying hard now, her words swimming in tears. I've heard Olivia cry only once before, when we watched *Charlotte's Web* at school. By lunch she was back to her smiley self. The difference now is clear in each sob, her pain reaching me through the phone.

"Where are you? Are you at home?" I start walking as fast as I can. It doesn't feel right using Max's money to call for another Uber, and it will take me thirty minutes to walk to the bus stop on the main road.

I check to make sure I have my Marin Transit Youth Pass. I'd started riding the bus to school at the end of last year to make it easier on Gram. Even so, nerves jitter low in my stomach. It's one thing to ride with other kids I know and another to ride by myself.

But Olivia needs me.

"Y-yes. Can you come?" Her voice cracks.

"I'll be there in an hour. I'm so, so sorry about your dad, Olivia."

"Text me when you get here."

"Okay. I'm on my way."

I hang up and keep walking down the gravel road. The sun beats down and melts my guilt until it sticks to me like taffy. How can I call myself Olivia's best friend? Since she never said anything about her parents fighting, I hadn't even tried to figure out what was bothering her. I always think of her as the one who needs all the attention. What if I'm the one who isn't happy unless it's all about me?

My boots rub against my heels. When I sit down on the bus, I pull one off and peel the sock off a newly formed blister.

I put my boot back on. I deserve the burning pain of it.

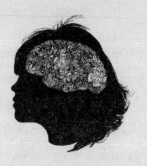

18.

Insula the Great

What makes humans different from animals? It wasn't until recently that scientists studied a part of the brain called the insula. They'd ignored it before, partly because it was tucked so deep inside the brain and partly because they thought it was unimportant. With MRI testing they discovered the insula is where we sense love and hate, gratitude and resentment, trust and distrust, truthfulness and deception. It allows us to show compassion and empathy. It's a huge part of what makes us human.

The Memory Keeper

Sometimes the things we think are unimportant are really the things that matter most.

I need my insula right now. I need to show Olivia all the compassion and understanding I've been keeping to myself. What good is my superpower of memory if I treat my best friend like she doesn't matter?

Olivia answers the door in sweatpants, and I almost don't recognize her. She hasn't brushed her hair, and it's tangled in a knot on one side of her head. Her eyes have dark purple circles. I don't know this zombie girl standing in front of me with hollow eyes.

"Hey," she whispers. "Thanks for coming."

I follow her up the stairs to her room. The house is quiet. Is there such thing as a black hole where all sound disappears? Even our steps are muffled by thick carpet.

"What happened?" I don't know if I'm asking about her parents or her room. Every piece of clothing Olivia owns covers every inch of space. There is no place to walk. I pick my way carefully, but she steps on her organza party dress as if it's not even there. I scoop it up and place it carefully on her desk. She may not care now, but she loves this dress.

"They've been fighting for a while. I guess they both had enough."

I sit on the edge of the bed. "I'm so sorry, Olivia. I can't even imagine."

Olivia wipes her tears with one of the folded T-shirts next to her. "Yeah, well. I've tried to pretend it wasn't happening. That worked well."

Her sadness spills out of her. It's in each piece of colorful clothing. It's in the overturned garbage can. It's in her tangled hair. It's in the pile of shoeboxes stacked like Legos in her closet.

When I hug her, she leans her head against my shoulder. "So, what did Max say?"

I sit back and stare at her. "Nothing really. Just that your parents were, you know, fighting."

"What did he say about your grandmother?" she clarifies, her cheeks turning pink.

"Oh!" I laugh nervously. "Sorry, I thought . . ."

"I read your texts," she says. "You said he wanted to show you something?"

"Yeah." I widen my eyes and hand over the folder. "This."

She opens it and stares at the blacked-out pages with a frown. "What the heck?"

I explain about the hacker and what the redacted file probably meant.

"Okay, so we need to solve this." She rips out a page from a notebook on her desk and grabs a purple gel pen. "Tell me everything you know. Leave nothing out."

"Olivia, we don't have to do this right now—"

"Nope, don't even try to talk me out of this. I need this right now. We're going to solve this, okay? Now, when did you find the journal?"

I get it. Helping me figure out Gram's past helps distract her from what's happening right now with her parents.

"Um, the journal? Oh, Gram mentioned it one day, and I got curious about what was in it. I didn't think it would be anything like this!"

Olivia looks up with a frown. "Wait? You stole your grandmother's journal for no reason?"

I sigh. I decide right then to tell her a small part of the truth. It's the least she deserves after the way I've treated her. "When Gram gets tired, she, um, gets this weird accent. I wasn't sure what it was. And she started telling me these stories about her childhood, but they didn't add up to what I've been told my whole life. I thought I should, you know, investigate."

"What stories?" Olivia puts her pen to the paper and waits.

I tell her everything I can without revealing the secret of Gram's memory. Or mine.

"What else?" She looks up expectantly. "Anything more tied to Russia?"

I squint. A niggle of something prods at one of my memory squares.

"What?" She waves her pen dramatically. "You're doing that thing where you blank out and then all of a sudden know a ton of stuff."

"Her doctor," I say in a rush. "Her doctor is a friend, and I'm pretty sure his name is Russian."

"What's his name?"

I close my eyes and toggle through the movie of yesterday. Gram was wearing her beige sweater with the blue butterflies. "Yakov is his first name, but that's all I know about him."

"That's not a lot," she mutters.

"I mean, I know where his office is, though."

Olivia rolls her eyes at me. "Duh, Lulu. That's huge!" She shoves her notebook and pens in one of her twenty thousand backpacks and tugs a brush through her tangles. "Come on, let's go."

"Where are we going?" But I already know. She's got that determined Olivia look in her eyes.

"His office! We're going to find out exactly how he knows your gram. What if he's the man from the woods?" She raises her eyebrows.

"He can't be," I say, but I'm not as confident as I sound. "She ran away from that guy. This guy is a friend."

"We'll see."

I hurry to follow her out of the house. "Shouldn't we tell your mom we're leaving?"

"She'll be asleep all day. Don't you want to know

more about this Yakov? If we can find out more about him, maybe we'll find out more about your gram. You want to know if she's a spy or not, right?"

"It's ten miles away," I say, ignoring the spy remark. I'm not convinced Gram used to be a spy, but Olivia's right. I do want to find out.

"That's what the bus is for. Duh, Lulu."

Once we're on the bus, I text Gram and Mom to tell them I'm with Olivia. Mom instantly responds with a kissy face and a string of hearts, but I don't hear back from Gram until we're almost to Yakov's office.

Gram: Give Olivia a kiss from me. I'm at home with Clay.

Me: And mom is there?

Gram: Yes, Lulu. Love u

I study Gram's text, wishing I could tell if she was okay. I hope she doesn't get too forgetful without me there to cover for her. I turn my phone over, determined to stop worrying about Gram spacing out in front of Mom. All I can do is try to find out what Yakov knows and hope it helps.

"Do you think you can get your gram to tell you

more stories?" Olivia asks. "All of them so far seem to be about her friend Jacob. Maybe you can ask where he is."

"I think it makes her sad to talk about him." I still can't stop thinking about the story of Jacob's father. How can a dad treat his family that way?

Olivia nods briskly. "Good. The sadder she is, the better. My mom always talks more when she's sad. We'll dig into Yakov and then see what else you can find out from your gram. I bet we solve this by the weekend."

And what does that mean? Finding out if Gram is a spy might still not help bring back her memory. I'm not sure I even want to know if it will change how I see her.

I swallow hard. "Are you sure you're up to this?"

Olivia's eyes narrow as she looks from the window to me. "Stop babying me. I'm fine. You're the one who needs help right now, not me. Got it?"

I nod, because I do know. I know Olivia needs to make new memories to replace the bad. Distraction is perfect for that.

My phone buzzes. "It's Max."

She rubs a hand across her face and grimaces. "Tell him I said sorry he had to see that last night. Talk about awkward."

Max: Hey

Me: Hey, I'm with Olivia. We're going to go find the doctor my gram went to yesterday. He might be Russian.

Max: Oh

Me: I'll tell you what happens

Max: Be careful.

Me: Olivia says sorry you had to see last night.

Max: No worries. Tell her I'm sorry it happened. I can meet up with you guys in a couple of hours if you want?

"He says to not worry about last night and he's sorry it happened. Also, he wants to meet up with us later?" I scrunch my nose.

"Maybe. We might need him to hack into his uncle's computer again."

Me: Maybe. I'll let you know

Max: okay

We sit in silence until our stop, then get out and walk in the direction I remember driving with Gram.

I want to go home and hug Gram and listen to Clay make plane noises. I want to watch Mom paint, and I want to play Boggle with Dad. I think about how, even though my family isn't perfect, at least they're still together. I don't know how I'd feel if I were Olivia.

I grab her arm and point to the one-story office building. "This is the place."

Olivia squares her shoulders. "Our plan is that we need donations for our school play. Got it?"

I follow as she barges through the front door like she owns the place. "Hello. My name is Piper Collins, and I am collecting donations for our school's play. Can I speak to your manager?"

I bite my lip to keep from laughing. Olivia is doing an awesome job channeling Piper's particular brand of haughty.

Two women are behind the front desk. One looks up and dismisses us, but the other smiles. "I'll go get Mr. Zhabin. Please wait here."

We wait for five minutes of excruciating silence until an older man lumbers out of the back office. He's huge—way over six feet—and is pretty much completely bald. The tattoos across his forearms are written in the same Russian Cyrillic as Gram's journal.

"Yes," he says in a thick accent. "Can I help you?"

Olivia launches into her volunteer story while I study him. Do I know him? Is this the man who chased us in the woods?

He senses my stare and frowns at me. "Do I know you?"

"Are you Yakov?" I whisper. I've lost my voice along with any courage I might have had.

"Yes. I am Yakov Zhabin. You look familiar. I know you, *da*?"

Olivia lets out a small squeak of terror. Her arm clutches mine, and her breathing escalates.

"I don't think so." I shake my head and smile. "We have to go. My friend needs her inhaler. She has asthma."

I turn and drag Olivia behind me. She wheezes impressively.

As soon as we're outside, she whispers, "He knew you!"

I glance behind me. He's staring after us. His giant form takes up the whole doorway. I can't get away fast enough.

"This was a terrible idea," I say. "I should never have let you talk me into this. What if he calls Gram?"

"Or turns her in to the government," Olivia says.

"Way to make me feel better." I start walking away as fast as I can without looking back.

Olivia glances over her shoulder, then pulls me behind the next office building. "I think he's following us," she gasps. "Run!"

19.

Amygdala

Our amygdala is an almond-shaped cluster of neurons. It's responsible for our memory of emotions, especially fear. It's our alarm system. Panic is a direct response to this fear. This is why Olivia and I run. This is why we don't stop until we're sure there's no way he followed us.

Olivia bends over and tries to catch her breath. "He was super creepy."

"Do you think he really was chasing us?" I look around to make sure we're safe.

Olivia stomps her foot and makes a low frustrated sound in her throat. "*Now* how are we supposed to find out what he knows?"

We walk in silence. At this point I'm not holding out much hope that I'll ever translate the journal. We catch the bus to my house and manage to find seats together.

Olivia sighs. "We need to tell Max. Maybe he can look up information about Yakov."

"I was thinking the same thing."

I text Max and give him Yakov's name and the address of his business. The late-afternoon sun shines through the bus window and my stomach rumbles. I missed lunch.

"He says he's on it," I say. "I'm not sure how long it will take, and I need to get home."

Olivia nods. "Good idea. You can get Gram to tell you another story."

"Maybe."

Olivia scrolls through her phone with complete focus. "There's a surprising number of Yakov Zhabins in the Bay Area," she says.

"There *is* a whole Russian neighborhood in the city."

"You mean Russian Hill?"

"I guess," I say.

"I think this one might be our Yakov." Olivia excitedly jabs her finger at her phone. "See— seventy-one years old and lives in San Rafael. That's close to his office. Maybe we should stake out his house?"

The bus lurches to a stop, and we hop off. As we hike up the hill to my house, I think about how different my life is now from how it was last week. If anyone said I'd be investigating an old Russian guy, I'd say they'd been watching too much television. And yet here I am, pretty much agreeing to whatever Olivia comes up with.

Clay's screams reach us while we're still three houses down. I recognize the pitch of his cries immediately and break into a run. I hear Olivia gasping for breath as she tries to keep up.

The open side door gives a clear picture of the kitchen. Clay is stuck in his high chair, his legs dangling at weird angles. He must have tried to wiggle out. I release the tray, and Olivia scoops him up.

"Lulu," he cries pitifully. He reaches his arms for me, and I hug him close.

"Where's Gram, little man?" I search each room, calling out for her or Mom.

"Bye-bye." His body shudders as tears stream down his chubby cheeks.

"No one is here," Olivia says, her eyes bigger than I've ever seen them. "They left him alone?"

I close my eyes, trying to calm down, and play back the scene of us rushing home. *Click.* "The van is still here," I say. I run out the front door, Clay's arms still wound securely around my neck. Gram sits in the driver's seat of the van, staring straight ahead.

I open the door. "Gram, are you okay?"

Her eyes are unfocused and swimming in a fog of confusion. "Where am I?"

"You're at home." I hold Clay back when he tries to hurl himself at her.

Gram shakes her head. "No. This is not home."

My stomach churns with fear. I turn and quietly hand off Clay to Olivia. She walks away, giving us privacy without my having to ask.

I rub Gram's hands between mine. Her skin is cold as ice, and I try to warm her. "Gram, you're home. It's me, Lulu."

I swallow my tears. It takes Gram longer than ever to come back to me. Seconds jump to minutes before she finally responds. Her eyes sharpen, and her mouth tightens like it does when she's mad.

"Where have you been, young lady?" she asks. "You didn't do your chores this morning."

I laugh in relief, but that only makes her angrier. If I'm not careful, she'll ground me before I can explain. "Sorry, Gram. I went to Olivia's. Her parents are maybe, probably, getting a . . . divorce. Her dad left last night."

"Oh no!" She cups a hand over her mouth. "That poor girl. It's a terrible thing for a child when her father leaves. Is she okay?"

"She's in the house with Clay. We just got home, and he was all alone. Where's Mom?"

Gram blinks. I wonder if her memory is anything like mine at all. If she has to flip through scenes of the day before she finds the right one. Or are the scenes out of order—with some erased altogether?

"Did I leave him alone?" Her voice is small and scared, so un-Gram-like that her fear leapfrogs to me.

"I have it under control," I say. "You need to stay with us until I have this figured out, okay? And you need to help me put the pieces together. Can you do that?"

"What pieces?" She lets me lead her back inside the house. Her feet shuffle as if she's even forgotten how to walk.

"Of your past, Gram. I need to help you remember."

I bring her to the couch, where Clay is curled up with his blanket. He scoots over to Gram and climbs into her lap. "Hello, sweetheart," she coos. "I'm sorry I frightened you."

I motion to Olivia to follow me to the kitchen. I

don't need to scare Gram more than she already is.

"What just happened?" Olivia asks.

"She doesn't remember things sometimes." I shrug and try to act like it's no big deal, even though my eyes still burn with unshed tears. Telling her feels like a betrayal to Gram. Can I really trust Olivia with this?

"Like she's losing her memory?" Olivia gasps and twirls around. "What if Yakov finds out? What if he, like, tries to shut her up before she says the wrong thing?"

"Why would he do that? We have no idea who he even is. He could just be a friend."

Olivia snorts. "A friend? You're kidding, right? He's way too scary to be a friend. He's definitely threatening her or something. Or maybe he's her handler, like Max said."

"Promise you won't tell anyone." My heart thunders as if we're still running from Yakov. What will I do if she says no? What will happen if everyone finds out? How will I protect Gram then?

She doesn't say anything for a long minute. I bite my lip.

Olivia finally nods. "Of course I won't. I promise."

Gram calls to me. I motion for Olivia to follow. Maybe with her here, I can put the puzzle together faster.

I sit next to Gram and reach for her hand. I try to show her with my smile that she's safe, that I love her. I need her to tell me what she knows, and I can't let my fear get in the way of finding the truth. "Let's talk about Jacob. You walked on the icy lake with him." I try to keep my voice from shaking. "Gram, was that in . . . Russia?"

I hold my breath as soon as the words leave my mouth.

20.

Dendrites

We have trees in our cells called dendrites. Well, not real trees, but they look enough like them. They're like tiny computers, multiplying the brain's processing power and bringing information to the cell body. If they aren't activated, then a memory might not be stored. The neurons (or brain cells) fire up depending on the thought or action going on, and an electric spark activates the neuron. If the dendrite doesn't receive this nerve impulse, then the memory isn't stored. We experience something, but we might not remember it.

✳ ✳ ✳

Gram nods automatically, her eyes out of focus. "Yes. In Moscow."

Olivia gasps, her eyes wide. It's one thing to make a guess and another thing for it to be true. Finally I'm getting somewhere.

"What happened with Jacob in Moscow?" I squeeze her hand.

Gram's voice takes on the same singsongy quality as before. "My mama worked at the American embassy. Sometimes she brought me so I could practice my English. She insisted I learn, but I couldn't tell Papa. He hated everything American—but he liked the extra money she made there.

"Her American boss, Mark, let me borrow as many books as I wanted. He was a good man—so kind. When Mama worked, I would read to her. I asked her if she thought Mark was nicer than Papa.

"'There is no one like your papa,' she said.

"It was true. My papa was so handsome that women stopped and stared at him when he walked by. But he never looked back. He only had eyes for Mama.

"After I helped Mama clean the last room that day, Mark got me ice cream and let me look at all the books in his library. They left me alone for a long time. Afterward I asked Mama where they were. She told me it was a secret—a secret from everyone—and the look she gave me was one I'd never forget. The other questions froze inside me, thicker than the ice on the lake.

"But I told Jacob—even though I wasn't supposed to—because I always told Jacob everything. He'd brought me cookies his mama made, the powdered-sugar ones I loved best. They melted in my mouth and made all the frozen secrets melt with it."

Gram smiles, her face transforming to one of delight. She reaches in front of her as if she is touching something. She keeps talking, caught up in the story she's reliving.

"He said it was to make me feel better, and I pointed to his split lip and his swollen cheek. I told him I was the one who should be trying to make him feel better. I could only imagine how much his cheek hurt and his lip burned whenever he spoke." Gram touches her cheek with a grimace.

"He said that his papa couldn't hurt him. And he said it almost as if he really believed it. I wanted to distract him from the pain, so I told him about learning English. I promised to help teach him, and he promised to keep my secret. I taught him the English word for 'friend,' and when he said it, he smiled past his sore lip. I knew then that I did the right thing, even though I'd promised Mama not to tell.

"After that Papa took me to visit Mama in the hospital."

"Your mama?" I ask with a frown. "Don't you mean Jacob's?"

Gram closes her eyes briefly. "Yes . . . yes, of course I meant Jacob's mama. I . . . I barely recognized her. Her jaw was broken and her eyes swollen almost completely shut. I cried for her, but I cried for Jacob more. He was all alone with his papa. He said he wasn't scared, but I knew he must be. I could see it in the way he flinched at every sound."

"Yikes," Olivia whispers. "Poor Jacob."

I widen my eyes at her and put a finger across my

lips, but Gram doesn't seem to hear Olivia. She continues with her story, her gaze briefly meeting mine.

"My mama's boss, Mark, came to my school soon after that day. He said he needed me to give Mama a message. He made me memorize it instead of writing it down." Gram pinches the bridge of her nose briefly, like she does when her head hurts. "When I gave Mama the message from Mark, she cried. I didn't know why then. I'm not sure I would have told her if I knew—"

A knock on the front door interrupts Gram. She looks up and blinks me into focus. "Answer the door, Lulu."

I grit my teeth and stomp to the front door. Max is on the other side with a huge grin.

"Hey," he says. "I found something."

I try to shake off my impatience.

He looks past me and nods at Olivia. "'Sup?"

Olivia pulls us into a huddle in the middle of the entryway. "Her gram is telling us about Russia. She totally admitted she used to live there."

I glance over my shoulder. The living room is

around the corner. "We should get back in there. I want to see if she'll keep talking."

"I can wait here," Max says.

"You might as well come in," I say. "She's going to ask who's here and then probably try to feed you."

Sure enough, Gram tries to stand when she sees Max. "Hello, dear. Come in. Are you hungry?"

Sorry, Max mouths to me as we follow Gram into the kitchen.

She's still shaky, so I stay close. "I think you should sit down," I say softly. "I can get Max something."

Gram starts to argue but suddenly goes blank. She stares off into the distance before she looks back at me. "Where's Jacob?" she asks in a little-girl voice. The one she uses when she tells me her stories.

Max's eyebrows disappear into his hair, and Olivia's eyes go wide.

"He's not here," I say, leading her to a kitchen chair. "Can you get her some water?" I ask Olivia. I sit next to Gram and keep hold of her hand.

Olivia hurries to the cabinet, whispering something to Max on her way back. I try to focus on

Gram and not on what they might be thinking.

"Jacob told me he's going away," Gram says in a hushed whisper. "His mama is leaving his papa. They can't tell anyone where they're going because Jacob's papa works for the government. If they stay in Russia, he'll find them anywhere they go. And he'll kill them. I know he will. I've seen the darkness in his eyes." She clutches at my arm, her nails digging so deep that I wince. But I don't say a thing. I let her talk.

"Jacob's my best friend. I can trust him with any secret I have. Who will I talk to now? Who will I trust?"

"You can trust me," I say, but I'm not sure she hears.

"Jacob promises to find me one day. We set up a way to find each other. A way no one will ever find out about. And one day we'll be together again."

A tear slowly trails down one of her cheeks. I look back at Max and Olivia, and both of them stare at Gram with wide eyes.

"Lulu?" Gram wipes at her tear. "Why am I crying?"

"You're crying for Jacob," I say as gently as I can.

She frowns and straightens into her normal ram-rod posture. Her gaze sweeps around the kitchen. "Olivia and Max. How nice to see you both. If you'll excuse me, I need to check on Clay. Who knows what the little terror is getting into."

Before I can protest, she pulls her hand from mine and hurries out of the kitchen.

"That was . . ." Olivia waves her arms around her like she's getting ready to dance.

"Super intense," Max finishes. He tucks his hands in his pockets. "You okay, Lulu?"

I shrug and pull out the notebook I keep on the counter. I begin to write down everything Gram's just told me. Just in case I forget. It isn't likely, but then again, I didn't think I'd find out my gram grew up in Russia and might be a spy. I'm not too sure of anything anymore.

I can sense Max and Olivia staring at me. I've tried so hard to keep this from everyone, but it's sort of a relief to have them know about Gram's memory. Both of them wait patiently for me to finish. Neither one makes a move to leave.

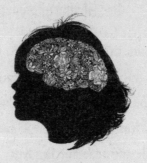

21.

Engram Cells:
The Brain Instagram

There are neurons called engram cells. Once these cells learn something new, they change, and then they go to different parts of our brains to hang out. Like when I was three and accidentally touched Mom's curling iron. My brain took a picture of the curling iron and posted it on my brain Instagram: my engram cells.

At first the engram cells in my short-term memory were the ones that reminded me to stay away from the long black thing plugged into the wall in the bathroom. Like when I post something on my story and it's only there for a day. But eventually the ones in my long-term memory remind me to use a glove and take my time when I curl my own hair. Like those pictures I took last year that will be on my Instagram until I'm old and in my twenties.

If I can find a way to tap into Gram's engram cells, maybe I can fix her. The trick is to figure out how to do it and keep her trust. I hope Max and Olivia will help.

Olivia smiles tentatively at me. "I'm sorry about your gram. I feel really bad about her friend Jacob. Do you think she ever saw him again?"

"I don't think so. My dad's never heard of him and I can't find anything else about him, but I haven't finished going through all the albums."

Max unfolds a paper he's fished out of his back pocket. "This is what I found out about that dude you met this morning. If you still want it, I mean."

My hand doesn't move to take it; I just stare at it like it's a snake that might bite me. Olivia takes it instead. "'Yakov Zhabin immigrated here from Moscow,'" she reads out loud. "'He was in the Russian military, then went to college here and started a successful import business. He has a wife and two sons.'"

Olivia looks up. "The army must be where he got all those tattoos. And it doesn't say he's a doctor."

"Maybe he's in the Russian mafia," Max says. "I'm pretty sure tattoos are their thing too."

"Duh, Max," Olivia says, hands on her hips. "Of course he's in the mafia."

"So, because he has tattoos he's in the mafia, and if Gram is from Russia, she must be a spy?" I shake my head. "I need proof. This isn't a game to me, you guys. This is my life we're talking about here."

Max watches me, his forehead wrinkled. "Whatever you need from me, I'll do. I like your gram. She's a cool lady. I just want to help."

Olivia scrunches her nose. "Sorry, Lulu. But I think we need to find out more about Yakov. You have to admit he sounds sketch. Don't you want to know for sure?"

"We could set up a meeting with him. Ask him how he knows your gram. See what he says," Max suggests.

"We ran away from him this morning," I say. "You don't think he's going to recognize us?"

Olivia leans against the kitchen counter. "Max can talk to him."

Max shrugs, a half smile lifting up a corner of his mouth. "That's cool with me."

I nod, my mind racing with possible meeting places. A detailed map of the park floats in the air above me. "If we meet at the park, I can bring Gram and Clay. They can stay at the play area, and Max can meet him at the duck pond. There's an area we can watch without being seen."

"How do we get Yakov there?" Olivia asks.

I spot Gram's phone on the counter next to her purse and get an idea. I swipe it and quickly find Yakov's contact information.

"Sending him a text from her phone," Max says with an admiring grin. "That'll work."

"What should I say?"

"See what your gram said the last time she texted," Olivia suggests.

I scroll down. "She asked him if they could meet. He said yes and told her to come to his office. There aren't any details or anything."

"Are there other texts?" Olivia leans closer.

"No. Just these." I start typing and show her when I'm done.

Meet me today at 4:30 at the Civic Center Park behind the duck pond. I'll be on the second bench.

"Ooh," Olivia says. "That's perfect. Just mysterious enough for him to be intrigued but not enough information to make him suspicious."

A small noise from the doorway has me looking up with dread.

"Lulu, why do you have my phone?" Gram asks.

22.

Medulla Oblongata

Our medulla oblongata sends messages between parts of the brain and the spinal cord. If the medulla's message gets intercepted, it can mean our brain forgets to control our breathing or our heart rate. It can mean the difference between life and death. Every spy needs a way to deliver messages— maybe it's a special word, a song, or a code that can only be deciphered with a particular book. If the message gets intercepted, then you're at the enemy's mercy.

* * *

By meeting with Yakov, am I putting Gram in even more danger? If she *was* a spy, was he the way she delivered messages to Russia? Or is it something else completely?

Too late to back out now. Yakov walks briskly down the hill to the second bench, looking around briefly before sitting. He gets his phone out and starts fiddling with it.

"Do you think he's texting your gram?" Olivia asks.

My heart leaps. "Go now," I say to Max.

Max walks past the bench before doubling back and sitting on the other end. Yakov glances over, and his bushy brows draw together. He sets his phone next to him on the bench.

I've left Gram and Clay near the slides. When Gram caught me with her phone at home, it hadn't taken much to convince her that I wasn't snooping. I told her that she'd left her phone in the kitchen and I was on my way to bring it to her. If she really is a spy, then her loss of memory must be affecting her skills. What kind of spy believes everything her granddaughter tells her?

"What's he saying?" Olivia whispers.

"How am I supposed to know? They're too far away." I take a picture to document the meeting. Max said it was important to record everything we could.

"I'm sorry about your gram's memory," Olivia whispers. "I know how much she means to you."

"She'll be okay."

Olivia bumps my shoulder with hers. "You know I'm always here for you, right? I'm like your Jacob."

I want to believe this. I don't want to think she'd ditch me if she found out about my memory. When we're together like this, it's hard to remember why I was so worried. Who else would follow a possible dangerous Russian guy with me?

I bump her shoulder back. "I know. Same."

But something still holds me back from telling her everything.

"He's waving us over," Olivia says, her voice wobbling with excitement.

I take a deep breath and step out from behind the tree. Olivia grabs my hand, and it makes Yakov's ferocious glare a little less scary.

"You girls again?" His gaze fixes on me. "I know you. You're Tatyana's granddaughter, yes?"

"Sue," I squeak. "My grandma's name is Sue. How do you know her?"

"Ah, yes, Sue. Of course, my mistake. Is Tat . . . Sue here?" He looks past me as if he expects to see her.

I shake my head and try not to look toward the play area. "You didn't answer my question. How do you know Gram? Why did she come and see you yesterday?"

He slaps his giant hands together. "So, you are a detective, yes? And these are your colleagues?" He gestures to Max and Olivia.

"We know who you are," Max says, his chest thrust out. "You better answer our questions or we're going to the police."

I catch Max's eye and give him a look I hope he translates as, *What the heck are you doing?* He shakes his head like he has it all under control. But from

Yakov's smile, I don't think Max knows what he's doing at all. Whoever he is, this man is a professional, and we're pests to him. Pests that he won't have much trouble swatting away if he wants to.

"And just who do you think I am?" His accent gets thicker, and it makes him sound like one of those bad guys in the movies my dad always watches.

"We don't know," I hurry to say. I'm not about to let Max ruin this whole thing. What if this is the only way I'll ever know the truth? "I just know she came to see you. And that maybe she wasn't born in France like my dad always said. I think maybe she was born in Russia."

Yakov pushes off the bench and stands up to his full height. Olivia and I back up a few steps. His arms look pretty long. I don't think he'd have too hard a time grabbing us if he wanted to.

"This is not my secret to tell," he says. "Tatyana . . . Sue must be the one."

"But what if she already—" I shut my mouth. If I tell this man anything about Gram, he could use it against her.

"Tell me why you're here, little Tatyana," he orders.

"Did you know her in Russia?" I ask, pulling myself up and meeting his stare. His eyes bore into mine.

His hand falls, and a part of his mouth twists in a half smile. "I think you learned your interrogation techniques from your *babushka*. She could always get answers from me. I will answer your questions when you are honest with me."

My heart leaps to my throat. I don't even know where to start. I point to his tattoos. "Where did you get those?"

He grins as if I've made a joke. "You are so much like her. She always knew how to pivot like a ballerina. How about this, little one? I will tell you this one thing. I received these tattoos courtesy of the Russian army. I am a retired soldier. Does that satisfy you?" He shakes his head and laughs. "No, I can see it does not. You want all my secrets, *da*?"

Max clears his throat. "Listen, man, Lulu needs answers. Can you understand that? If you really care what happens to her grandmother, then you'll tell her what you know."

Yakov glances at him before turning his full attention back to me. "I do care about your *babushka*. This is why I cannot speak to you until I talk to her first."

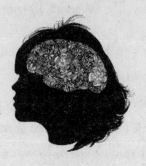

23.

Cerebrum

The largest part of the brain is the cerebrum. It's folded in ridges and valleys, and if you flattened them out it would take up about two and a half square feet. We really need our brains to be all wrinkled or they would never fit inside our skulls.

Now that I've flattened out the problem with Yakov, it's way bigger than I first thought. I'm never going to get it to fit back into the neat place it was before we came up with this stupid plan. Now Yakov is going to tell Gram. What if the stress makes her memory worse? It seems like every time she talks about her past, she gets more . . . unfocused.

"It's me," Yakov says, and then speaks rapid Russian into the phone. His eyes narrow on me while he talks.

I may not understand Russian, but I have a pretty good idea what he's saying to Gram right now. Max smirks his trademark smirk, and I start to see it isn't him being a jerk at all. It's what he does when he's nervous and not sure what to do.

Yakov pockets his phone and points to me. "Stay here, little one. Your *babushka* is on her way."

"Great. Just great," Olivia mutters. "We're busted."

Max shifts from one foot to the other. "Maybe we should get out of here?"

"She knows we're here," I say. "How will running away help?"

He looks over his shoulder and grimaces. "I guess it won't, but she sure looks mad."

I bite my lip to keep from smiling at Max's terrified expression. It almost makes the sight of Gram storming down the path worth it. Almost.

"What do you think you're doing, young lady?" Gram sets Clay down and faces me with both hands on her hips.

Yakov chuckles. She switches her glare to him. "How is this funny?"

He holds his hands up in the air. "Not funny. No funny here."

She turns back to me. "Why did you drag Yakov out here? What is going on with you?"

"He isn't a doctor," I say, latching on to her lie to make me feel better about mine. "You said he was, and he isn't."

"How do you know this?" She shakes her head as if she doesn't recognize me, but it isn't her memory this time. It's disappointment.

"I made her look him up," Olivia says, her face pinched with worry. "She told me about your visit, and I . . . I . . ." Her eyes widen to saucers when she can't think of a story that fits.

Clay chooses that moment to fart so loud that Gram jumps. I slap a hand over my mouth to stifle a giggle, but it escapes and ends in a high-pitched cackle.

"I hear a moose," Yakov says with a bark of laughter.

Gram's mouth twitches, and a smile escapes when Clay declares, "I fatted."

"Say 'excuse me,'" she instructs. He immediately obeys and then crouches next to a pile of rocks. Sorting rocks is Clay's passion.

I'm still giggling nervously when she turns her attention back to me. "I'm still waiting for an explanation, Lulu," she says.

How much should I tell her? She seems to trust Yakov, but does that mean I can too? I try like crazy to get my giggling under control, and I finally stop long enough to take a deep breath.

"I was worried about you," I say. Do I tell her what I know? "You lied about his being a doctor, so I wanted to know why."

The shift in her is visible. Her hands slip off her hips, and she hugs herself.

"I used to be a medic," Yakov says. "In the Russian army. I can't practice here, so I start a business like a real American. Sue knows this, so she asks me to look her over. She is fine. Nothing to worry about, little one."

"Yes, yes." Gram nods hard enough for me to know this is all another lie.

Why? Gram doesn't seem afraid of Yakov, and there's a certain familiarity between them. Her being a spy actually makes the most sense, no matter how much I don't want it to be true. No one here is telling the truth, except for Clay and his farts.

"But—" Olivia starts to argue. I grab her arm and she stops.

"I'm sorry, Gram. I'm so glad you're really okay. Thank you, sir, for helping her." I flash my best polite smile and hope Yakov buys it. If he is a spy, then he'll be able to tell if I'm pulling one over on him. But who ever suspects a kid of anything?

"Thank you for being so understanding, Yakov. You know how young girls can be, yes?" Gram says with a flutter of her hands.

Yakov flashes her a wry smile, and they seem to communicate without speaking for a second before he says, "*Da*. I understand. My own granddaughters would be the same, I think."

"You still haven't explained how you know him," Olivia says. Her face turns dark red when we all turn to look at her. She avoids my gaze as she continues. "I mean, how did you meet?"

Gram's hand shakes as she fixes the one curl that always falls over her forehead. Yakov steps closer to her, as if he's trying to protect her. I cringe. I'm supposed to be helping her, not hurting her. She shouldn't need protection from me.

"You can tell me later, Gram," I say in a rush. "Let's go home. Clay's hungry, and Olivia needs to get back."

"Tat . . . I mean, Sue helped me learn English when I first moved here. We met in college." He winks at Gram, who is still shaking like a leaf.

"Yes." Gram's lips twist into a semblance of a smile.

"We stayed very good friends over the years." Yakov takes both Gram's hands in his. He seems to infuse her with his strength, and her trembling slowly stops. Gently, he kisses her hands before letting go.

"Pretty handsy handler," Olivia whispers, her eyes wide.

I nod. Was this part of how they kept their real relationship hidden?

Gram smiles warmly at Yakov. "We've taken enough of your time. Please say hello to Margaret for me."

He returns her smile before turning to me. "You're a good granddaughter to try to protect your *babushka*. I hope we meet again, Lulu."

I'm not sure what I hope any longer. All I can do is keep pretending I have it all under control.

24.

Hypothalamus

The hypothalamus is responsible for making most of our hormones. The ones that make you feel like you're on a carnival ride spinning so fast that you're not sure which way is up. I guess some of those hormones are necessary for life—just think what would happen if we didn't have them. None of us would grow, or feel happy or sad. But if my hypothalamus weren't so excellent at its job, I wouldn't care that Gram is still lying to me.

✳ ✳ ✳

We drop Olivia off. She looks happy to be home, which says a ton about how awkward the car ride was. "Don't give up," she whispers before hopping out of the car and running toward her house.

"I don't like you going behind my back, Lulu," Gram says, cool as can be, and I shrink in my seat a little. She doesn't look at me when she talks, and there is nothing hesitant or feeble about her.

"Sorry." I don't know how to reach her. She's in take-charge-Gram mode. This Gram doesn't think anything is wrong with herself. This Gram is just fine. But how long before she leaves Clay alone in his high chair again? Or forgets how to get home?

"I met Yakov when he defected to America," she finally says. "Back in those days, you couldn't just fly to America; you needed to escape."

"How did you get out of Russia?" I hold my breath. Will she tell me?

"My mother worked in the American embassy. One of the assistants to the ambassador helped get us out. He sponsored us when we got here."

"Mark?"

She brakes so suddenly, my neck whips forward. "How do you know his name?"

I pick my words carefully. "You told me. You've been telling me stories about growing up there. Don't you remember?"

Her breath comes faster. She shakes her head, and the car jerks to the right a little before she corrects it.

I point to the side of the road. "I think you should pull over, Gram."

She listens, her hands trembling when she puts the car in park.

"Let's sit here awhile," I say in my calmest voice. "Clay's asleep, so we can just stay here until you feel better."

Gram drops her head to the steering wheel. "I feel a little dizzy."

"You tell me to take deep breaths when I don't feel well," I remind her.

She sucks in air and lets it out slowly. I want to ask her a million questions, but I don't.

"When I was very little," Gram says, her eyes

looking past me, "maybe just a little older than Clay, my papa took me with him to visit one of his friends. They were all drinking, and I asked if I could have a sip. Papa thought that was hilarious, so he gave me a drink." Gram smiles, but it doesn't touch her eyes.

"It burned like I'd swallowed fire. I coughed and coughed so much, I almost threw up. Papa's friend said I must not take after him, but I wanted so much for Papa to be proud of me. So I asked for another taste. This time I forced myself to swallow the drink and not cough. My eyes wept like waterfalls, but I refused to cough. I smiled and told them how good it was. And Papa laughed. He was so happy that night, and I was happy to be with him. Next to him."

I barely breathe as she talks. I can't imagine my dad ever acting like that. "Why didn't your dad come with you to America?" I ask when I'm sure she's finished her story.

"When I first came to America, I was so confused." Her hands flex on the steering wheel as if she's still driving. "I missed Russia. I missed my papa more than I imagined. I wrote him a letter telling him to please come soon. I told him about our new house with a yard. How I can have as much bread as I want. How the weather is always warm. How I made a new friend, Margaret, and she was teaching me how to ride horses. How we lived next to the beach and that I had a bowl full of sand dollars on my dresser.

"But I knew I'd never send this letter. That Mama wouldn't wish me to. I knew it, but I wrote him letters anyway and then ripped them up."

Gram shakes her head and rubs a trembling hand over her face. "I don't want to talk about this anymore."

I glance back at Clay's innocent face while he sleeps. "You don't have to, Gram. We can just sit here for a little while and talk about whatever you'd like."

"You have nice friends," she says. She leans her head back against her headrest and closes her eyes.

"Yeah, they're awesome," I say.

"Even Max?" she asks, her mouth curving slightly upward. She looks over at me.

"I guess, yeah. He's not as bad as I thought. He's pretty cool, actually."

"And pretty cute, too, yes?" Her eyes crinkle with humor.

My face heats up. I open my mouth, but nothing comes out.

Gram takes pity on me and changes direction. "And Olivia? How is she holding up with her parents separating?"

I unbuckle my seat belt and twist sideways so I'm facing her. I thought about Olivia's underlying sadness and how her usual happy smile seemed forced. "I don't know, and I don't know what to do to help."

One of Gram's eyes droops a little like it does when she's tired. "Just be there for her. Listen. That's what a good friend does."

"I'm trying," I say. "But it feels like I should be doing something more."

Gram nods. "Jacob said just knowing I was there if he needed to talk was enough." She pauses and smiles. "I thought after Jacob that I would never have such a good friend again. But I learned in life you make many friends—some better than others, but all of them important."

"Like Margaret, who taught you to ride horses?"

"Yes." Gram's smile slips into a tight line. "She was my first friend in America."

"How long were you friends?"

"That's another story," she says. "And a boring one."

"I doubt it, Gram. You don't know how to be boring." I smile my best smile.

She grabs my chin and pinches it lightly. "You think you will charm me into telling you all my secrets, yes? I suppose you will, my sweet girl."

"Did you meet her when you first moved here?"

Gram closes her eyes for a second before she answers. "Before I met Margaret, I poured all my thoughts into my journal. It saved me, to be able to write anything I was feeling. Mama would no longer let me speak Russian, so my journal was the only place I could still *be* Russian."

I squirm in my seat. The journal that saved her is currently under my mattress.

"Back then Russia and America were enemies," Gram continues. "Mark told us we should say we were from France. Our passports were French, and my mom taught me how to fake the accent. I met Margaret the first day of school, and she loved that I was French. She made it her job to show me how to be an American girl. She even taught me to wear makeup so my mama couldn't tell." Gram waggles her finger at me. "So don't think I can't tell when you and Olivia wear mascara."

I giggle. It's weird to think of Gram as being my age once.

"She told me what a period was and that she'd had hers for a year. I was horrified that such a thing would happen to me! I know you understand, Lulu. How scary it can be to have your body change when there is so much else around you changing too. There are always too many things happening at once, and it can be overwhelming, yes?"

I nod. I want to grow up, but sometimes I don't like what that means. Gram was the one who showed me what to do when I first got my period. She told me it wasn't something to be afraid of, and her no-nonsense, practical way of looking at it made it less scary.

"Yes, I see you understand," Gram says with a smile. "When it finally happened to me, my mama showed me what to do and welcomed me to woman-hood. But I didn't want to be a woman. I didn't want to have this happen every month, but Margaret said it would get easier. And since there was nothing to do about it anyway, I might as well accept it. Embrace it, even. But it was one more change in a sea of changes I didn't ask for."

"Tell me about it," I mutter.

Gram reaches out and squeezes my hand. "But I loved American school! I loved how the teachers let us read any book we wanted. My favorite was *Jane Eyre*. She overcame so much and still hoped for love."

"I love that book too," I say. Gram was the one who bought it for me.

"Yes, I know you do. I'm happy that we have such similar tastes," she says. "I loved exploring my school library and learning about anything I wanted to. It was glorious to have such freedom. I did worry that if I changed too much, Jacob might not recognize me when we finally reunited."

"Or your dad?" I ask softly.

"Yes." She smiles sadly. "I think I knew my papa would never leave Russia, but I still missed him. But eventually my mother remarried. My stepfather was the man who helped us get out of Russia."

"Mark?"

"Yes, he was a very good man. He made Mama happy. But I worried if Papa ever heard about it, he might think I'd given up on him too."

"Oh, Gram," I say in a rush. "I'm sorry."

She waves her hand like she does when I catch her watching TV shows that make her cry. "It is done. No reason to be sorry. I think it's time for me to drive us home, yes?"

Gram seems steady enough. It feels weird, like I have to give her permission to drive, as if I'm now the adult. But the time talking about her past doesn't seem to disorient her—it seems to do the opposite. Maybe the good memories help her and the bad ones upset her.

She pulls the van out on the road, and I stay quiet so she can concentrate. I don't think she and her mother came here to spy after all. I think her mother came here because she was in love with Gram's stepfather, Mark.

Relief hits me in waves. I didn't realize how much it bothered me to think of Gram as a spy. As someone I never really knew. But now I can't wait to get back to the photo albums and see what else I can find. If Gram isn't a spy, then maybe I've been looking for the wrong memory this whole time.

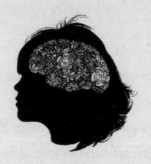

25.
Glial Cells: The Stars of the Show

Glial cells make up more than 90 percent of all human brain cells, but because they don't have the nerve impulses neuron cells have, they used to be ignored. It turns out they're pretty important. Star-shaped glial cells, called astrocytes, actually influence how the brain processes information. They are thought to control which messages get sent and when. Without them we wouldn't be able to learn anything new. Without them we couldn't change our minds.

* * *

When we get home, Clay is a cranky beast. He is the worst when he wakes up from a nap. I leave him and Gram alone in the kitchen, where she plies him with snacks. She seems to be doing okay, so I have some time to look for clues.

I pull the boxes of albums into the middle of my bedroom. I put aside the ones I've already looked through and start on a new pile. A glossy pink one is filled with baby pictures of Dad. It's like looking at Clay but with old-fashioned clothes and shoes. The next three albums are packed with photographs of trees and mountains. Finally, I hit the jackpot with a weathered brown leather album. Inside are pictures of Gram when she was in high school.

I study a family picture of her with her mother and my great-grandfather Mark. Her mother and Mark have their arms around each other and huge smiles on their faces. Gram looks like a movie star with her glamorous makeup and dark hair.

The next few pages show a vacation to the coast, but the last is of Gram and another pretty girl with blond hair pulled into a high ponytail. I trace a finger over her face, and I wonder if this is Margaret.

Another picture stands out. This one is of Gram with a man who, at first glance, I think is my grandfather. I look closer. It can't be Grandpa Daniel—this man is much taller. He towers over Gram. I can't see his expression since he's staring down at her, but whoever it is, it's clear he cares about Gram. Maybe it's in the careful way he leans over her, like he's protecting her, or how he can't look away to even smile at the camera.

Did Gram date someone before Grandpa Daniel?

My phone buzzes next to me with a text from Max.

Max: Hey, just checking to see how you and your gram are doing after all that.

Me: It actually turned out okay. She told me some more stories. And you're wrong about her being a spy. I think the reason they moved here was because her mom was in love with an American who worked at the embassy. Maybe that's why he helped them get out of the country.

Max: Did your gram tell you that?

Me: No. I think they kept it secret from her.

Max: Sounds like you just don't want to believe your gram is a spy. I'm never wrong about this kind of thing.

I roll my eyes. It's comments like this that remind me why I used to think he was such a jerk.

Me: They got married, like, literally, right after they moved here. I don't think Gram wants to think her mom would do that. But maybe deep down she knows?

Max: But how do you explain the French passport and this Yakov dude?

Me: My stepgrandfather got them into the country by saying they were French, so that's why she has a French passport. And Yakov is a friend she met in college. I bet she was drawn to him because he spoke Russian. It was a way to speak the language again.

Max: Maybe. But he's kind of scary, right? He's huge. Not someone I'd picture your gram being friends with.

I start to answer when it hits me. Yakov *is* really tall. I grab the photo album and study the picture of the man with Gram. Could this be Yakov? It's hard to tell since his face is turned away, and this man has a ton of hair and a sweater that would cover any tattoos on his arms.

Me: I think I found a picture of them together. The weird thing is it sort of looks like they're a couple. Like in love or something.

Max: Yeah? Weird—they don't look like they'd match.

I close my eyes and try to rewind the day to when we were at the park with Yakov. I don't know what it is, but I feel like I'm missing something important.

I snag the scene at the park and open it. It plays in front of me—each word, each gesture. I get to the part where Gram tells Yakov to say hello to Margaret for her.

That's it!

Me: Okay, so I just sort of remembered something. My gram told Yakov to say hi to Margaret. And then on the way home, my gram mentioned one of her first friends here was named Margaret. Do you think it's the same person?

Max: It might be. I don't know many people with

that name. But I guess it might be someone else. If it is the same girl, that would mean he married her friend but was in love with her? That's serious messed-up drama right there.

I giggle, imagining Max's smirk as he types this. I flip through the rest of the album in search of more pictures of the mysterious tall man, but I don't find any.

I'm about to tackle a new album when Dad hollers that dinner is ready.

Max: Ask your gram about Yakov and the picture.

Me: Haha. You like the drama ☺

Max: He could still be her handler and they fell in love, but they couldn't do anything about it because of orders. I still think they're spies. No offense to your gram—she's awesome. Do you remember your memory of the woods and the man yelling she's a traitor? And what about how it would get her one day? Explain that. . . .

I don't answer him. He's right—I can't explain that yet. I'm quiet during dinner, waiting for the perfect time to ask about Yakov. Gram laughs and teases

Dad. Clay hides half his food under his plate, and Mom paints in the air with her finger.

Mom once told me she sees colors everywhere. At any given time, she can mix them and pull them together to create art no one else sees. When she does it, it looks like she's conducting an imaginary symphony. Even when she's away from her studio, she can create masterpieces in the air around her.

"What does it look like?" I ask, suddenly curious. What's it like to make art out of everything you see? Is that why it's so easy for her to shut people out?

Mom startles, as if she's forgotten I'm there. I nod to her invisible painting, and she smiles. "It's of you and Clay, of the time we went to the zoo a month ago."

"You mean five months ago," I say. "On the first Wednesday, January second, and it was a free day. It rained the first ten minutes and we bought an umbrella, but then it stopped so we didn't need it after all."

I look up, and Dad and Mom are staring at me with identical expressions of surprise. My stomach drops to my toes. *What did I do?*

"That can't be right," Mom says. "I thought we went only a few weeks ago."

Gram smiles encouragingly. She wants me to trust them. They're my parents after all, so maybe they won't think I'm weird.

Yeah, right. Sure they won't.

"I think Lulu might be correct," Dad says, scrolling through his phone. "I remember I was going to buy the tickets and I didn't have to because it was free. Yep, here it is. I made a note of it because that was the day before I went to that conference in Berkeley."

Mom's eyes go wide. "That's amazing, Lulu! What are the odds you'd remember with such detail? I think you have a little of my artistic eye, don't you?"

I open my mouth to tell them it's so much more, when the doorbell rings. Dad shoves his chair back with a sigh. "Sorry, guys. I forgot that Ben wanted to go over his thesis."

Mom frowns. She hates when he brings work home. Funny, since she works on her art constantly. "Ask Ben if he wants some dinner."

Dad kisses the top of Mom's head as he walks

by. In a way I'm relieved for the distraction. I don't know if I'm ready for anyone else to know what I can do. And honestly, why should I trust them with my secret when I can't even trust them with Gram's?

Gram picks up Clay's plate and tsks at all the wasted food around it. She seems perfectly normal. Better than ever really. And I want to believe everything will be okay. That the memory loss is no longer a problem and our family will stay just like this forever.

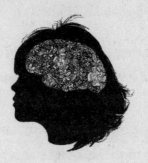

26.
Thalamus: The Inner Chamber

Can you imagine never sleeping? Located deep within the cerebrum is the thalamus, which is an inner chamber that helps the brain stem, spinal cord, and cerebral cortex send messages to one another. One of the things it does is regulate sleep.

Total insomnia is what happens when a person can't sleep. There are studies that say that without sleep, you'll die within six months. One person, who tried to break the record of the most days without sleep, started hallucinating within eleven days. For kids I bet it happens even sooner.

The darkness presses all around me. My dresser seems to loom in the shadows as if it's ready to come alive and eat me. It's close to three in the morning, and my thalamus is not doing its job. I blame the excitement of today. The park, Yakov, Max and Olivia's belief that Gram must be a spy—all of this has caused my thalamus to misfire.

I give up trying to sleep and reach for my phone to use as a flashlight. I tiptoe down the stairs to the kitchen. Whenever I can't sleep, I snack.

Gram's light shines beneath her door. Another person whose thalamus isn't working properly. I knock lightly, and the door swings right open. Gram stares past me, her eyes wild and unfocused.

"Margaret, why are you doing this to me?" she says, tears streaming down her cheeks.

I place a hand on her shoulder and try to ignore my heart, hammering in my ribs. "Gram, it's me," I whisper, glancing over my shoulder. I can't let my parents hear her like this.

"You lied to us. You told Jacob I didn't love him. You told him I was marrying Sam. Why did you do that? You ruined our friendship. You ruined our lives." Her cries quickly turn into sobs.

I close the door behind me and lead her to the bed. "Gram, it's okay. You're okay."

She huddles on the bed. I climb next to her and hug her tight. "He loves me," she whispers. "He wants to marry me. Why did you trick us? I can't marry him now. He keeps begging me to, but I can't. You knew I wouldn't do that to you."

"Gram, it's me. It's not Margaret. It's Lulu."

She slowly stops crying and looks up at me. "Lulu?"

"Yes, it's me. You're at home and you're safe."

"I'm home and safe," she repeats, one more tear escaping down the lines of her cheek.

"You need to go to bed, okay?" I help her under the covers and tuck them around her chin. Her eyes close, as if her eyelids are too heavy to keep open for one more second.

I kiss her forehead as she's done so many times for me.

"He loves me," she murmurs, her eyes still shut. "He still loves me."

"Who, Gram?"

"Jacob," she answers sleepily. "But I can't marry him. Not when he's married to Margaret." She snuffles in her sleep, and a rhythmic snoring quickly follows.

I slip back upstairs without getting my snack and stop at Clay's room. He sleeps in his crib with his butt up in the air, his Pull-Ups sticking out the top of his monster-truck pajamas. His breath comes out in even puffs, like he's trying to blow out a candle.

I climb over the edge of the railing and curl up next to him. He throws an arm across my neck, and I don't even care that he smells like pee. The rhythm of his heart rocks me until I finally fall asleep.

I wake to a low voice saying my name, and I focus in on Dad's face looking down at me. "What are you doing in here?" he whispers. He moves Clay to the side so I can climb out.

"He had a nightmare." I can barely look at Dad. I can't tell him that I'm the one who was scared and lonely. I can't tell him that his mother is slowly losing her memory and I can't seem to do a thing to stop it.

"All that talk about the zoo last night at dinner made your mom nostalgic. She and Gram are taking Clay to the zoo today. I'm sure she'd love for you to join them."

What if Gram has one of her memory episodes in front of Mom? The panic of last night swells like a tidal wave in my blood.

I quickly get ready and run down the stairs.

"Can I ask Olivia and Max if they want to go to the zoo?" I ask as soon as I get to the kitchen. "I, um, think it might help Olivia, you know, take her mind off her dad leaving."

Gram looks up from where she's doing the cross-word puzzle at the kitchen table. "What a lovely idea, Lulu. You're such a good friend."

The image of her frightened and crying last night

is in a shimmering square in front of me. My stupid memory seems to be using it as a screensaver that I can't take down, and I want to crawl into her lap and hug her tight like I used to when I was younger.

Dad swallows a sip of coffee. "Who's this Max you speaketh of?"

"Just a friend."

He looks to Gram for a longer explanation. "From the stables," she says helpfully. "He helps his dad train horses and teach the riding classes. A very sweet boy."

"Does Rose know him?" He frowns like he does when he's worried about Mom. "She had a rough night last night. A lot of people might be too much for her."

"I don't even know if he can come," I say. It's not like I had the best sleep last night either. What about me? Or Gram? Why is he always so worried it will be too much for Mom?

"Go ahead and ask them," Gram says. "I'll entertain the kids and let Rose just enjoy taking pictures of the animals."

Dad takes another gulp of coffee before tightening the lid on his travel mug. "Your call. Let me know if you need me."

Once he leaves, I text Olivia and Max. I glance at Gram. She bites the side of her cheek as she writes in a word. Does she remember anything about last night?

"Want some breakfast?" Gram asks with a smile. I love her smiles. They fill her entire face and make her eyes almost disappear.

"Yes, please."

She laughs and pushes away from the table. "So polite. That's my girl. Pancakes sound good?"

"Yes, please," I say with a grin. She tweaks my cheek and turns toward the cabinets.

Her phone sits next to my plate. A text pops up from Yakov.

Yakov: Does your granddaughter know the truth?

27.

Neurotransmitters

There are gaps between neurons, or nerve cells, and neurotransmitters are chemical messengers that communicate between the nerve cells. Without enough of the neurotransmitter acetylcholine, brains start having difficulty with memory and attention. It's like reading a text message meant for someone else. The meaning gets lost without someone to explain it.

Does your granddaughter know the truth? What the heck does that mean? I stand up and then sit back down. I roll Yakov's sentence around, take a deep breath, and try to calm down.

"Gram, do you still keep in touch with your friend Margaret?" I ask, a vague idea forming. "The one who taught you how to ride and put on makeup?"

Gram slides a plate of pancakes in front of me. She's made a blueberry smiley face, and all I want to do is cry. Gram knows I hate blueberries; it's my dad who loves them. I pick them off quietly to avoid making her feel bad.

"Margaret and I lost contact over the years."

I pour a river of maple syrup over the top to kill any lingering blueberry taste. "But weren't you super close? What happened?"

"Are you fishing for another story?" She narrows her eyes at me. "Is that what this is?"

"Story!" Clay shuffles in holding his stuffed pig. "Pancakes and story!"

Gram puts her hands on her hips and smiles down at him. "You too? Hop up in your seat."

Clay climbs into his chair. I put his tray on and slide one of my pancakes onto the plate Gram hands me. He picks up a piece and shoves it in his mouth, syrup sticking to his fingers. "Story," he says, his words muffled around the food filling his mouth.

"You heard the boy." I shove a forkful into my mouth and smile my best please-Gram-tell-me-everything smile.

She sighs as she sits next to me. "Why are you so curious about Margaret?"

I shrug and look down. "You might have said she lied to you and Jacob. How he loved you but she tricked him into marrying her."

"Oy vey," she mutters, rubbing her eyes. "When did I say all that?"

"Last night. You were sort of upset. Do you remember?"

Gram frowns and stares past me. "I remember that Margaret's idea of friendship and mine were very different."

"Story," Clay shouts.

"No yelling," she says automatically.

I put both hands together and pout. She rolls her eyes, but I can tell I've won her over.

"I think the thing I miss most about Russia, believe it or not, is the weather," she says slowly. "I miss the crystalized cold of the winters and the white nights of the summers. I could think clearly there. The cold here is wet, and it seeps into my pores. I love it now, of course. Now I see the fog and think of it as something good. It keeps us from getting too hot and nourishes my flowers."

She waves her arm. "But back then everywhere I looked was fog and rain, and it seemed to mirror my heart. I would take long walks in the redwoods to feel closer to Russia. The trees reminded me of the forest my papa would sometimes take me to when I was a little girl. The trees there were so tall, it was as if their branches brushed the sky."

Her face turns up like she sees the tops of the trees right here in our kitchen, and I can't help but look up too. When all I see is our white painted ceiling, I close my eyes. I picture the tall, straight trunks of a redwood with a small patch of green as high up as the clouds. I try to imagine how Gram felt so far from the home she grew up in.

"Trees." Clay nods and keeps eating.

"One day with my papa," Gram continues, "the clouds beckoned me. I thought if I could climb high enough, I could touch them. Perhaps even sit on one. So while Papa took a nap, I climbed."

She laughs and shakes her head. "But, of course, the branch snapped, and I fell and broke my arm. Papa woke up to me howling. He scooped me up and drove to the hospital faster than I've ever been in a car since. It's a miracle we didn't crash. My arm mended, but I sometimes dream of the pain. The sharp ache while it healed. This was how my heart felt when I first lived here. It ached for my old life in Russia, for Jacob, and for Papa."

Gram rubbed her arm. Is she homesick even now?

"Ouchie?" Clay points to Gram's arm, his eyes wide with concern.

"No ouchie," I say. "Gram's okay."

Gram doesn't seem to hear him. She continues talking. "When the ache overwhelmed me, I'd close my eyes and see Jacob's face like a picture. But after a while the picture began to fade. I couldn't see the shape of his nose or the color of his eyes. I was afraid when I finally saw him again, I would no longer recognize him. Would he know me? Or would we be strangers?

"I waited for years to see him again. I worked hard to get into the college we agreed on before I left Russia. The only American college we'd heard of—Harvard."

I lean closer. "How did you know Jacob would get out of Russia?"

"Indeed," Gram says with a shake of her head. "We had big plans but no way to know if any of them would come true. I had no way of knowing if Jacob would be there. We set up the plan so long ago, and I worried he might have forgotten or not been able to defect. I waited every day. I wore a red sweater, as planned. I did it all, but he wasn't there. Then one day I was sick and couldn't go until later in the afternoon." She pauses dramatically. "And there he was!"

I grin and clap. "Yes!"

"I knew him the moment I saw him," she says with a small laugh. "His hunched shoulders and bushy black hair. My Jacob. His voice was deeper, and he was even taller than before. But he insisted he recognized me instantly too. He said it wasn't my red sweater that gave me away, but my beautiful face." Gram laughs again, reminding me of Olivia when she holds her mouth to keep in a giggle. "The flatterer."

"Like when you guys played chess," I say with a smile.

"Yes," Gram says, her own smile fading as she continues. "Our friendship didn't skip a beat. He told me about the brutal time he had after I left. How he'd lost his mother when he was sixteen. I hated to think of how alone Jacob must have felt. He said he survived by hoping for the day he would see me again."

I want to ask about her papa, but something stops me. She stares out the window, far away with her memories.

"I told him about my life here in America," she

says. "But it felt wrong to talk about my happiness here when he had struggled so much. Even here it was still hard for him. He'd been in the army since he was sixteen."

"How did he leave Russia?" I ask.

"My stepfather, Mark, used his influence to bring him here. I will always be grateful to him for so many things, but that most of all."

"Did you love Jacob?" I'm pretty sure I know the answer, but I want to hear her say it.

"I did," she says in a low voice that shakes with emotion. "I loved him. I'd always loved him, but I thought he only saw me as a friend. I was afraid he'd never love me the same way."

By now, I'm pretty sure I know who Jacob is. I just don't know why Gram didn't end up with him when they were so obviously in love.

I'm trying to think how to ask Gram when Clay shrieks, "Mommy!"

"Good morning, everyone." Mom sails into the room wearing a flowered sundress and a floppy hat. "Are you going with us to the zoo, Lulu?"

I shrug. Couldn't she have waited five more minutes before barging in?

"She is," Gram says. "I think Olivia and Max will be joining us as well, yes?"

"Zoo!" Clay pounds both fists against his tray. "Tigas!"

Mom wets a paper towel and wipes Clay's sticky fingers. "You want to see the tigers, sweetie?"

My phone buzzes, and I look at all my missed messages. I'd been so caught up in Gram's story that I forgot to check my phone.

Olivia: I'm in. Mom says she can drop me off in ten minutes.

Max: Have to teach a lesson. Can you and Olivia swing by later, though? I'm waiting on something that might be interesting. Don't worry—I didn't break the law.

Me: What???

Max: I'll tell you when I know for sure.

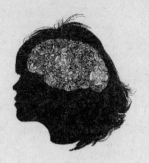

28.
The Outer Zone of the Cerebral Cortex

The biggest part of the cerebrum is the cerebral cortex. It's made up of the famous gray matter you hear so much about. This "outer zone" of nerve tissue determines how smart you are and what kind of personality you have. But the coolest thing about the cerebral cortex is that parts of it will take over for another part if it's needed.

Just like how Gram took over for Mom and how I'm trying to take over for Gram. We help one another out. That's how a family works.

✳ ✳ ✳

"The text said what?" Olivia hisses.

A man in a blue cap bumps into me before I can respond. "Excuse me," he murmurs before heading toward the popcorn truck.

Clay tugs on my hand. "Churro," he chants over and over. We're waiting to buy some, and the line is moving at a glacial pace. It's more crowded today than usual. The fog has burned off and the sun shines down on us, making me glad I wore shorts.

"Almost there, bud," I tell him as patiently as I can. He comforted me last night. The least I can do is not get annoyed at him asking for the same thing twenty million times. I look back to Olivia.

"The text was from Yakov. He asked if I knew the *truth*."

Her eyes widen so much, I worry they might pop out of her head. "The truth? That your gram is a spy?"

"Nope." I shake my head. "That's not it. I think the truth is that Yakov is actually Jacob from her stories."

"What! Why do you think that?" Olivia pays for her churro and takes a huge bite. "Mmm." Her eyes shut as she chews. "This is worth smelling disgusting animals all day."

"It just fits," I say. "There's the picture of the tall guy who was totally in love with her. Then Gram tells me this story about how Jacob found her again in college and how he hid all his tattoos so he wouldn't scare the students. Sound familiar?"

Olivia wipes sugar off her chin. "Didn't Yakov say they met in college?"

"Yes! See? I'm not sure why he'd change his name to Yakov, though."

"Because he's a spy?"

Clay drops his churro, and his lip trembles. I quickly hand him mine. He shoves it in his mouth with a happy gurgle. "Why is your answer always that the person is a spy?" I say, louder than I need to. "I'm trying to tell you that isn't what's going on."

"I get it. You don't want it to be true. But it might be."

A quick burst of impatience hits me. "Just because

your dad left—" I quickly shut my mouth, but not before the arrow hits its target.

Olivia's face falls, her eyes slicing me with her pain. I wish I could rewind the last few moments and take it back.

"I'm sorry, Olive."

She shrugs and blinks furiously to keep from crying.

Clay spots Gram and runs to where she's sitting. Mom walks ahead of us, taking pictures of everything that captures her fancy.

"I love your gram," Olivia says over the shouts of a crowd of kids from a summer camp. "But just because she's great doesn't mean she isn't a spy. You saw the redacted files Max had. There's too much evidence for you to just ignore it."

"You guys ready to go see the tigers?" Mom's voice reaches us from ahead. Her smile is tired. She never does well in crowds. She glances at a little girl whose curls spiral around her face like Maisie's used to.

"Tigas," Clay screams.

"Here's your milk." Gram hands him his cup and

flashes Mom a concerned look. "Why don't you rest here, Rose? We'll go see the tigers and come back for you."

Mom nods. "Thanks, Sue."

We wind our way through the crowd. I glance back to see which bench Mom chose when I notice a man behind us. He looks vaguely familiar, with dark hair covered by a dark blue baseball cap. I whip back around and grab Olivia's arm.

"I think there's someone following us."

"What?" She cranes her neck around.

"Don't look! He'll see." I pull her until we're right behind Gram and Clay.

Once we've entered the tiger enclosure, I look around again. The man stands in the back checking his camera.

"The man in the blue hat and gray sweatshirt. He's got a camera around his neck. I saw him when we first got here, and he bumped into me when we were getting churros. He's always behind us, and he's definitely watching us."

Olivia stretches and pretends to tie her perfectly

tied sneakers. When she stands back up, her face is flushed. "He's totally watching us! Do you think he's CIA? Or a Russian spy sent to see if your gram is talking?"

I don't even try to argue. I don't know what to believe anymore. "I wonder if she knows him."

"Ask her," Olivia says, her mouth hanging slightly open as if she's had the idea of her life. "They're always talking about strangers and trusting your gut. Tell her your gut says this guy is a weirdo and he might be a kidnapper. If she knows him, she'll try to talk you out of it."

"I don't know." I want to ignore him and hope he goes away.

"If you don't do something, then we might never know." Her eyebrows go up, and she jerks her head to the side where he's still standing. "He might be here to hurt her."

I take one more peek. He lifts his camera to take a picture of the tigers and swings it slightly in our direction.

I pick up Clay and turn so the man can't see my

face. "Gram, there's a man following us. He just took our picture."

She frowns at me, her eyes flicking over my shoulder to where Olivia points. "He's probably just part of one of these groups."

"He's been everywhere we've been today, and he keeps taking pictures of us. Trust me, he's definitely following us."

Gram glares at the man. "Let's find your mother," Gram says, grabbing my hand and then Olivia's.

We walk fast with the man still behind us. "See," I say when Gram glances back.

"Yes. I see." Her mouth is in a straight line of pinched lips, and she looks forward with worried eyes.

Mom is leaning back on the bench where we left her. She stares at the clouds with a dreamy smile on her face.

"Rose, there's a man who appears to be following us. I think it would be wise to alert the authorities here at the zoo. He might be a predator."

"A tiga," Clay shouts. He's a lot smarter than he looks, this brother of mine.

"Really?" Mom looks around, her mouth a perfect circle. "Point him out."

"The man with the camera wearing a blue hat," I whisper.

Mom shakes her head. "He looks harmless."

"Gram, please," I say, turning to her in protest. "He was following us."

Gram's mouth flattens even more. She turns back and points at the man. "You there! Are you following my grandchildren?"

The man lowers his camera and points to himself.

"Yes, you," Gram says. People around us stop and look.

"Sorry." The man waves the camera at her. "I'm a photographer for the zoo. It's my job to take pictures."

"Prove it," Olivia says.

Mom looks startled at Olivia's challenge and steps away from us like she's embarrassed. But Gram nods to him, waiting for his proof. He reaches into his pocket, takes out an ID card, and gives it to her.

"I usually wear it around my neck, but the string

broke," he says. "I'm really sorry if I scared your little girls."

Olivia clenches her fists. I grab her arm before she can do anything stupid. "I think he's really who he says he is," I whisper.

"Still doesn't mean he can get away with calling me a little girl," she hisses.

Gram frowns at us before addressing the photographer. "We are sorry for the misunderstanding. Perhaps you might consider getting your ID fixed before following two young girls around?"

Olivia turns to me with a grin. *Go, Gram*, she mouths.

The man frowns. "Look, I said I was sorry. If you'd like, I can give you some of these pictures for free."

"You frightened all of us," Gram says, pulling Clay and me closer. "That's unprofessional at the very least. I think you owe us more than free pictures."

"Lady, I don't owe you nothing." The man's face goes from pink to red.

"I'll be speaking to your manager." Gram pockets his ID.

The man's mouth hangs open. He looks over his shoulder at the crowd gathering.

"Sue, maybe we should just go," Mom whispers.

"He threatened my grandchildren," Gram says, not even trying to keep her voice down.

"Look, lady. I'm sorry." The man holds out his camera. "Please, look at the pictures. You can have them all."

Gram sniffs. "No, thank you. My daughter-in-law is a wonderful artist. Her pictures are far superior, I'm sure."

"Fine. Whatever. What can I do to make it up to you?" The man starts to look desperate. He shifts uncomfortably as Gram stares at him.

"Apologize and promise not to do it again," she says with a sigh.

"Sorry," he mutters. "I won't do it again."

Gram shakes her head and puts her hand to her ear like she couldn't hear him. Olivia snickers.

"I'm sorry," he says, this time in a clear voice. "I won't do it again."

"Very well." Gram nods and hands his ID back to him. "You may go."

I hug her arm tight as we watch him leave. The crowd begins to scatter.

"Gram," I say, my eyes wide with admiration. "You were amazing!"

"You're a total superhero," Olivia declares. "I wouldn't want to fight you."

"Superman!" Clay reaches for Gram.

Mom stands quietly off to the side. "You were very brave, Sue," she finally says, but there's something to her tone that doesn't ring true.

"You were the best." I kiss Gram's cheek. Mom's silent judgment makes me want to reassure Gram even more.

As we head to the car, Olivia leans in. "I don't think that guy was really a photographer for the zoo. I'm just saying."

I look back and see him standing by the edge of the gate, staring after us.

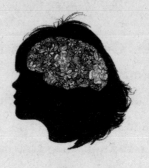

29.

Axon

Axons take information away from the cell body. These nerve fibers make up the pathways in the brain. Without them there are no connections, and no connections means no memory.

What makes Gram remember details of growing up in Russia but forget how to get home? Why can she remember every detail of Jacob's appearance but forget who I am?

* * *

The man following us must trigger something in Mom. A maternal side she'd buried underneath a mountain of depression and acrylic paint. As soon as we get home, she leaves Clay with Gram and Olivia in the kitchen and pulls me to the side. We huddle in the hallway near Dad's office, and she takes my hand in hers. Her eyes swim with tears, and I look down at our hands so I don't have to see her cry.

"Lulu, I know I haven't always been the mom you needed," she says, her voice catching. "Today at the zoo, Gram was incredible, and I saw how much you and Clay rely on her. When there was trouble, you turned to her." She bites her lip and tries to compose herself.

I frown. Gram's the one who is always there for Clay and me. It shouldn't come as a surprise that we'd turn to her when there was trouble. "You didn't stand up for us. She did."

Mom sighs shakily and nods. "I deserve that. But I can see that I need to step it up and listen to you more. I remember how hard it is to be almost thirteen. I want you to know how much I love you. I've loved you from the first moment I knew I was pregnant. You do know that, right?"

"Yes, Mom." I clear the irritating scratchiness from the back of my throat. It feels strange to have her staring at me like this. Like I'm the only thing that matters.

"I think you're ready to hear this," she says, and just like that, she has my full attention. Ready to hear what? I lean closer, and she lets out a breath as if it hurts to speak. I'm almost afraid of what she's about to say.

Does she know about Gram's past? Is she going to finally answer all these questions buzzing in my head?

"I've been struggling since your sister died."

Mom takes another deep breath and looks down at her hands covering mine. It's all tangled veins and fingers. Like a framework of muscles and bones tied together in a strange patchwork of grief.

"I was so happy when I found out I was pregnant with your brother. Having Clay helped a little," she continues, glancing back up at me. "But sometimes women can get really depressed after they give birth. And, unfortunately, this happened to me." Watery, smudged lines paint her face, but her voice is steady. "My art helps me make sense of how I'm feeling. It helps me forget the pain and focus on something beautiful. I find pieces of myself every time I create something, and it's easier to fit back into . . . reality, to make myself whole again. I know what's important, and I'm trying really hard to get better."

I don't know what she wants me to say. Does she really think I don't know she's been depressed? Does she think I don't care? Would it matter if I told her how much I do care?

"Say something," she urges. "You can say whatever you want."

I wonder if that's true. Saying whatever I want seems too much. Like looking at my memory as a whole instead of breaking it up day by day. Maybe, with Mom, I should do the same thing. Take one thing at a time and go from there. I know what it feels like to miss something I used to have and wish

I could get it back again. How, sometimes, I feel alone even when there are people all around me.

"Is depression like how it feels to be lonely?" I finally ask. It might seem like a small thing, but the question is mired deep in my heart.

Mom's eyes shimmer with tears. She grimaces, and the pain etched in the spiderweb lines around her eyes deepens. "Oh, Lulu, hon. Have you felt lonely?"

I shrug and swallow past the weird hollow spot in my throat.

She squeezes my hand harder. *Click.* A memory box shimmers in front of me. Ten years ago. Mom holds my hand, and Maisie is on her lap. She's telling me a story about the best big sister in the world, and I know she's talking about me. Her eyes are filled with love for Maisie, but when she looks up, the same love is there for me, too. Her hand is tight in mine. She promises to never let go.

The memory closes. I file it away to the time before Maisie died.

I tune back in, catching the end of what Mom is saying. "Because I love you and Clay so much. I promise, I *am* going to try harder. I know you have a very special relationship with your gram, and I don't want to get in the way of that at all. But I want you to know I love you. I'm so very sorry I stopped being the mom you needed."

With each word, I see a hint of the strength behind her fragile beauty, and I want to believe her. Hope is like a butterfly softly fluttering along my cheeks.

"I love you, Mom," I say. My words feel new, as if I'm unfurling the fist I've held tight for so long and offering her my open hand.

"I love you too, Lulu." She smiles past the tears still falling. "I wish you could remember me when I was a good mom."

"I do."

She shakes her head. "I mean before . . . before Maisie. I was a way better mom. I promise."

"I know what you meant." *Should I tell her about my memory?* For the first time, I feel like she might actually understand. Like she might be okay with it. And then maybe I could tell her about Gram, and we could figure out what to do together.

My phone rings and buzzes noisily in my pocket. I pull it out and glance at Olivia's text.

I told Max about the creeper at the zoo. He says he wants us to come to the barn. How long is your mom going to talk to you?

I wave my phone. "It's Olivia."

Mom wipes the back of her hand across her eyes. "Clay is probably driving her crazy. We can talk more later."

She links arms with me, kissing me softly on the forehead before we walk back to the kitchen. I cling to her hand; now that I have her, I don't want to let go. I don't want to leave this bubble that's around us. I'm afraid the second I step outside it, Mom won't see me again.

Olivia hops off the counter, her eyes wide. "Max texted and we need to get to the barn. There's a special lesson that is . . . special."

"I can take you," Mom says. Her arm is still firmly linked with mine.

Gram frowns. "Do you have a lesson today? Did we miss it?"

"It's a special lesson," Olivia repeats, smiling her most innocent smile.

"It would be great if you could drop us off," I say to Mom, trying to ignore Gram's confused expression. "You should bring Clay. He always conks out in the car. That way Gram can rest."

"How's that sound, little man?" Mom tickles Clay and swoops him up for a kiss.

He's fast asleep by the time we pull up to the barn. Mom smiles. "You know your stuff, Lulu. The best big sister in the world."

"Don't worry about picking us up," Olivia says. "My mom said she would."

Mom waves as she pulls away, and I can't help the twinge of guilt I feel for lying to her. She hasn't tried this hard in a long time. Maybe things are really going to be different.

"You look weird," Olivia says.

I pull my hair out of a ponytail and let it fall over my face. "My mom and I just had a really good talk."

Olivia slings an arm around me. "That's awesome. Are you going to tell her about your gram?"

"I was thinking about it."

"I think you should make sure your gram's not a—"

I wait for her to finish, but she clamps her lips together.

"A spy?" I finish for her.

"Sorry. I know you don't like when I say it."

We're halfway to the back of the barn when Max steps out of one of the stalls. He leans the shovel he's holding against the wall. "Hey."

Olivia grabs the shovel before it can drop to the floor. "What's the big thing we needed to rush down here for?"

Max hands me a paper. "This is what I found. I did a quick search when I went to walk my uncle's dog." He sees my look and holds both hands in the air. "Hey, it's not my fault if he leaves the screen open and his password never changes."

"What's on it?" Olivia hangs over my shoulder.

I unfold the page to find a grainy picture of Gram when she was younger. *Tatyana Petrov* is written underneath, along with a phone number.

30.

Occipital Lobe

Your eyeballs are directly connected to your brain. The occipital lobe (still not an earlobe) helps us understand what the eyes are seeing. If the occipital lobe were damaged, we could still see, but we would have no idea what we were looking at.

"Earth to Lulu." Max waves a hand in front of my face.

"This is a picture of Gram. It's the same as the one in her Russian passport."

Olivia hooks her arm through mine and looks

closer at the picture. "She kind of looks like you, Lulu. So weird. Do you think the phone number is Russian?"

"It definitely looks international."

"I know what to do," Max says. "Follow me."

Olivia trails after Max, dragging me along. "Where are we going?" I ask.

"Dad's office. He left to go buy a horse and won't be back until tomorrow."

"Why are we here?" I ask. He shuts the heavy wood door, and the scent of horse spray and leather fill the small, musty room. There's a beat-up desk in the middle of the room and two spindly wood chairs on either side of it.

"I say we call the number," Max says, hopping up on the desk and picking up the ancient tan phone next to him. "Let's see who picks up."

"And then what?" Olivia scoffs. "Since you're so fluent in Russian and all."

"We can ask for information about Tatyana Petrov," Max says, leaning forward and staring right at me. "Come on, Lulu. I know you want more answers. This might be the way we get some."

I blink, blood pumping through my veins in a loud ocean of noise. Do I want to know? Is it better to know, or is it better to pretend? If I could go back to when Gram was just Gram, would I do it?

"Okay." I stretch the paper out on the desk. Gram seems to stare at me as if I'm betraying her. "Call it."

"Wait!" Olivia paces from the desk to me. "What if they trace the call to us? Will we get in trouble? I'm too young for prison!"

"Chill," Max says with a grin. "This number is to the barn. We do tons of business with people in Europe. There're some crazy-valuable horses here. We can just say we dialed the wrong number or something."

"Not if you ask about Gram by name," I remind him.

He picks up the phone and raises his brows expectantly. "They won't know it's us."

"But what if it hurts her?" I point to Gram's picture. "What if we get her in trouble?"

"With who? You keep insisting she's not a spy." Max shrugs. "We don't know if we don't try. How can you help her if you don't know who the enemy is?"

Olivia claps her hands nervously. "Just call already. Right, Lulu? We'll totally help you if this goes wrong."

"Okay," I whisper, the familiar ache in my stomach kicking up from mildly nauseous to might-puke-any-second-now.

Max punches the number in and waits. "It's ringing."

"How weird," Olivia says under her breath so only I can hear. "A phone that rings."

"He's helping," I whisper, too nervous to laugh.

"Hello," Max says. "Who is this?"

He hops off the desk and walks as far as the cord will allow. Olivia and I move closer so we can hear. A man's voice booms so loud, Max holds the receiver away from his ear.

"Do you speak English?" Max shouts.

"He's Russian, not deaf," Olivia mutters.

"A little," the man answers, the words faint but distinct. "You are American, *da*? Only American will call me in middle of night. Good for you that I'm old man and don't sleep much." The man chuckles and then coughs for several seconds.

My eyes go wide. "The time," I whisper. "What time is it there?"

Olivia looks at her phone. "One in the morning?"

"Sorry about that, sir. May I ask who this is?" Max asks, this time in a normal voice.

"Sir, may I," Olivia whispers mockingly.

Max rolls his eyes, and I motion for her to stop.

"You called *me*," the man says once his coughing stops. "But I will answer if you tell me who you are."

Max points at the phone with a questioning look. "Um, a friend of someone we think you might know."

There's silence and then. "This is Alexei Petrov. Now you will tell me what this is about."

Max holds the phone out to me. "Ask him."

I breathe deeply and take the phone. "Mr. Petrov? Did you ever know a Tatyana Petrov?"

"Da—yes. She is my niece. She lives in America now."

Olivia's mouth drops open. "What even?"

Max motions for me to keep talking.

"Um . . . Do you . . . ? Um . . . Are you still in contact with her?"

"I will need to know who I speak with before I answer this. Is she well?"

"Um . . ." *Do I tell him?* Max nods. Olivia nods. "I'm Tatyana's granddaughter."

There is silence for a second before the man's voice booms loudly in my ear. "This is little Lulu? I am your great-uncle Alexei! Tatyana told me all about you and your brother."

"Oh! Um, it's nice to meet you." Sweat beads along my forehead. What do I ask a long-lost uncle I never even knew existed?

"It's nice to meet you?" Olivia whispers in disbelief. "Why would you say that? Ask him about your gram!"

I wave a hand in front of my face. I can barely concentrate with his heavy accent. I don't need her and Max judging every word I say.

"You must come visit me in Russia!" Alexei exclaims.

"Uh, why did my grandmother and great-grandmother leave Russia?" I ask quickly.

The line crackles with static and silence. I'm afraid he's hung up. "Hello?"

"You must ask Tatyana," he says abruptly. "But I can tell you it was for good reason. I did not know where she was for very long time. After many years of silence, she finally could call me. We had much to catch up on."

Why would no one tell me anything? First Yakov and now Alexei. What was the big secret?

"But the thing is," I say, my gaze meeting Max's, "she's sort of forgetting things. I thought if I could learn as much as I can about her, maybe I could help her remember."

Max looks down and kicks at the metal edge of the desk. Olivia comes and puts her arm around me.

Alexei mutters in Russian before he says in English, "I am most sorry to hear. This is what happened to Olga. It is very sad. My poor Tatyana. I would love to answer all your questions. Unfortunately, my wife is insisting I go back to bed. You will call me again, *da*? When it is not middle of night."

"I'm so sorry for calling you so late. I promise, it won't happen again," I say. "Just one more thing. Is Tatyana's papa still in Moscow? Do you have a phone number for him?"

"*Nyet.* My brother died a couple of years ago. *Khorosho, chto izbavillis'.*" He spits the words out.

"Oh," I say, my mind reeling with all the information. I don't know Russian, but whatever he said sounded bad. Like he was really angry.

"I look forward to talking more another time," Alexei says in a calmer voice. "*Dasvidanya, moya dorogaya.*"

"*Dasvidanya,*" I say, trying out the Russian word for goodbye.

"*Ochen khorosho*—very good," Alexei says. "You are a natural."

I give the phone back to Max, and he hangs it up.

Olivia claps her hands together. "Well, that was interesting."

Max rubs the back of his neck and meets my gaze. "I'm sorry about your gram. That day at the mall?"

I nod. "She forgot where she parked."

Olivia looks at Max and then at me. "Oh—is this what he helped you with?"

"It's when I finally knew I had to do something. I've been researching how the brain works, and I think there's something in Gram's past that is triggering her memory loss. Something really traumatic. If I can find it and make her face it, she can heal and her memory will get better."

Max frowns. "How do you know that will work?"

"I don't," I say. "But I have to try. She's my gram, and I owe it to her. I owe her everything."

"We'll help you," Olivia says, motioning to Max. "Won't we?"

"For sure," Max says. "I mean, we know she moved here from Russia and kept it secret. That could be because she's a spy." He puts his hand up to stop my protest. "I know that's not your favorite theory, but we can't rule it out. It would explain a lot. And maybe it's the key. What if the memory is about one of her missions?"

Olivia holds up a finger as she counts down what we know. "She left Russia for mysterious reasons. There's a file on her that's redacted. And then there's the Russian guy in the woods who called her a traitor."

"I have a different theory," I say. "We also know my gram's mom is the one who insisted Gram lie, and that she married an American who worked at the American embassy in Russia. I think Gram's mom fell in love and wanted to leave her husband. In those days you couldn't do that without getting in big trouble. That's why she had to sneak out and lie so the Russian government couldn't find her."

Olivia takes out her phone and types furiously. "You think the files are redacted to hide them from the Russian government? Do you think—" She looks up at me. "What was his name?"

"Mark," I reply.

"Yeah, Mark." Her thumbs fly as she adds in more information. "Do you think Mark had the power to do that?"

"Maybe," I say. "I kind of want to talk to Yakov again. Alexei said Gram had a good reason to leave. If it's more than her mom falling in love with Mark, then maybe Yakov will know."

"Ooh," Olivia says, jumping up and down. "Tell him your theory about Yakov being Jacob."

Max grabs a baseball cap off his dad's desk and puts it on. "Who's Jacob?"

"I say you fill him in while we go to Yakov's. I still have his home address." Olivia waves her phone.

"Let's go out the side door. If my dad's overseer sees me, I won't be going anywhere," Max says.

We fill Max in on the details about Jacob while we walk to the bus stop. The fog drifts in, cooling the air and making the long walk easier. Max and Olivia walk on either side of me, and I can't imagine doing any of this without them or why I thought I needed to. They've seen my memory at work and are still here, backing me every step of the way. With their help, I know I can figure this out and help Gram.

My HSAM chooses to kick in halfway into our walk, replaying the conversation with Gram's uncle Alexei.

The memory plays slowly, word by word, and I keep stopping over one detail in particular. When I told Alexei about Gram's memory loss, he mentioned that the same thing happened to Olga.

Who was Olga?

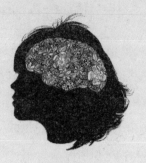

31.

Soma

The cell body, or soma, is where all the magic starts. The dendrites and axon branch off of the soma. Without it you have nothing to build on. Sometimes you have to go back to the beginning to understand where you ended up.

We climb on the bus and scan our Marin Transit Youth Passes. The bus is packed, so Olivia sits in the first available seat. I grab one a few rows back, and Max sits across from me.

"We should have a plan," he says. "He might try to keep stuff from us again."

"Not when I show him this," I say, holding up the journal I've been carrying around with me.

"What is that?"

"My gram's journal," I whisper, and tuck it away quickly. It feels wrong waving it around on a crowded bus, and I feel a little guilty for even mentioning it.

Max points at the book. "Why are we going to Yakov's, then? Just read it."

"I can't."

"I mean . . . I get it. You don't want to be a loser and read her private thoughts or whatever. I know I sure wouldn't want to read about my grandma when she was young." He scrunches his nose like he smells something gross. "But, dude, I think you're going to have to. It might have the answer you're looking for."

I shake my head. "No, I mean, I can't because it's in Russian."

"Oh." He looks out the window as the bus slows. "Yeah, that's a problem. You going to let Yakov read it?"

"I might if he really is Jacob."

The bus drops us off a couple of blocks from his house, and we spend the walk talking about how we're going to handle Yakov.

"Soften him up first," Max instructs. "Then you can hit him with the one-two knockout. Find out who he really is."

I'm as ready as I can be when Yakov opens the door. He's wearing a Kiss the Chef apron that barely covers his stomach. Somehow it makes him look even more intimidating.

"Ah, little Tatyana," he says with a jovial laugh. "You are persistent, *da*?"

"Are you Jacob?" I blurt.

"Way to lead up to it," Max mutters under his breath.

Olivia shoves his arm. "Shut it."

Yakov frowns down at me, but it's not a scary frown. It's more of a sad frown, his eyes shining with something I noticed the last time he saw Gram. Protective, but filled with love. Like how Gram looks at Clay and me.

"Yakov is Russian for Jacob," he acknowledges.

"But only one person ever calls me Jacob. I think you know who, *da*?"

I show him the journal. "I need to know about Gram's life in Russia. I know there's a secret— something I'm missing. You're a loyal friend to her and her oldest friend. I even know your dad was a monster and that she was the person you turned to when he took his anger out on you and your mom. She told me the stories."

He glances back inside. "Come with me," he says, stepping outside and closing the door behind him. He stalks around the side of the house, motioning for us to follow.

"He's taking us to where he tortures his victims," Olivia whispers.

I elbow her and glare.

"She might be onto something," Max mutters, eyeing the narrow path between the tall hedge and outer stucco walls of the house. We're completely secluded from the road.

I roll my eyes. This is Gram's Jacob. He's not going to hurt us.

Yakov ushers us into a small office off the side of the garage. It's surprisingly airy, decorated with leather couches and a huge mahogany desk. He points to a couch. "Sit."

I perch on the edge, my fingers tapping nervously against the back of the journal. I can't let him brush us off again. I need to know. He puts his hand out for the journal. I let it go, my grip tightening on the edge before he takes it. Yakov flips it open to the first page and starts to read.

Olivia grabs my hand and squeezes it. Max leans forward like he's ready to grab the journal if needed.

"Does your *babushka* know you have this?" Yakov asks. He leafs through the rest of it, lingering on the later pages before abruptly closing it.

"No," I admit. "But there's something she hasn't told you." I take a deep breath, not sure if I should continue. But if he loves her, I have to trust he'll help.

Yakov motions for me to continue. "Go on, little Tatyana. I am listening."

I continue in a rush of words. "There's something wrong with her memory. She's forgetting things, and if I can find out what happened to her in Russia, I know I can help fix her."

"We all forget things," he says with a sigh. "Some things are better forgotten."

"Not if they're why she's losing her memory in the first place," I argue. "I've been doing research. There are times where our brains experience severe trauma, and it can cause amnesia. If I can find the memory that's causing the trauma, then I can help."

Yakov glances at Max and Olivia. "I think I will talk about this with you only."

Olivia stands up and grabs Max's arm. "Come on, let's get some air."

Max grumbles under his breath but follows her out the door. "Call out if you need us," he says over his shoulder.

"You have good friends," Yakov says. "That is extremely important."

"I have *great* friends," I agree. "And I guess you know how important that is since you and Gram were best friends for so many years."

Yakov sits at the chair next to his desk. His look

of concern draws his bushy eyebrows together. "I love Tatyana. I will always love her. You can trust me with the truth about her."

I take a deep breath and let my words out in one long stream. "She sometimes can't remember where we live or who I am. I can't leave her alone with my little brother because she wanders off without him. I'm afraid to let her drive unless I'm there to give her directions. I'm afraid one day she'll leave and forget how to get home."

He closes his eyes, pain etched in the deep grooves along his mouth. "Ah, Tatyana, my beautiful one. Why didn't she tell me?"

"She's scared," I say. My voice echoes in the small room. "She won't admit it, but I can see it. She's done everything for Clay and me—I have to make this better."

"There are some things that can't be fixed, no matter how hard we try."

A knot in my stomach pushes against my ribs. My legs begin to shake. "I don't believe that. Just because you gave up on her so easily doesn't mean I will."

He opens his eyes and stares. "Is that what you think? That I gave up on her? I left the country I love *for her*. I offered to give up my marriage *for her*. No, little one, I never gave up on her. She gave up on me."

"Why did you marry Margaret if you loved my gram? You both worked so hard to find each other again. How could you marry someone else?"

He sighs. "My biggest weakness is I always wanted my Tatyana to be happy. I would do anything for this. When her friend Margaret tells me that Tatyana wants to date another boy but is afraid of hurting my feelings? I am hurt, yes. But more importantly, I want Tatyana to have everything she wants. I don't want her to be with me unless she loves me as I love her. Margaret says the only way to push Tatyana to date this boy she likes so much is if Margaret and I start to date."

I let out the air I've been holding in a rush. "She tricked you!"

"*Da*, she tricked me. I think Tatyana's friend is so sweet to make sure she is happy. At my wedding to

Margaret, I am confused when I ask Tatyana where her boyfriend is and she tells me she isn't dating the boy anymore. She is crying, so I think it's because the boy broke her heart."

"But it was because she loved you and you married someone else. Did she tell you?"

He shakes his head sadly. "No, she would never do that. Margaret confessed it to me. Her conscience finally bothered her and she wanted me to know why she'd done it. That she loved me."

I want to cry for my gram and this giant of a man in front of me. "But why did you stay married to Margaret? She lied to you."

A look of pain flickers in his eyes. "Tatyana wanted me to be nobler than I am. She begged me not to betray my promise. To be loyal to one's promises—it was everything to her. So I stayed married to Margaret. But if your *babushka* would have said yes, we would be together right now."

"What does Margaret think?" I can't help but feel sorry for his wife—the woman I thought I hated only minutes ago. It's funny how fast feelings can change when you know the whole story. I'm still mad at Margaret for betraying Gram. But I feel bad that she's married to a man who will always love another woman.

"We never speak of it." His laughter is tinged with bitterness. "She prefers it that way."

"What happened in Russia? I think I know why Gram and her mom left the country. Was it because my great-grandma fell in love with Mark?"

"You don't give up, little Tatyana," he says. He rubs his hands together. "I will tell you one thing, but she won't like it. She will never forgive me if I break her confidence."

I wrap both my arms around myself. "It won't matter if she can't remember you. You need to tell me so I can help her. Please."

Yakov opens a drawer and takes out a picture of a young girl scowling at the camera. "This is your *babushka*. This is how I remember her when I close my eyes and dream of Russia."

I bring it closer. She looks exactly like me. I meet his eyes and smile.

"Her stories to you are not all true," he says. "You said she told you about my father. My father died when I was a baby."

I put the picture down, my heart drumming in my ears. I don't understand what he's saying. If Gram wasn't talking about Yakov's father in her stories, then who was she talking about? "Why would she lie about your father being a monster?"

"Because the monster wasn't my father," he says slowly. "It was hers."

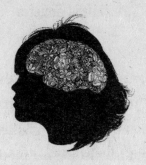

32.

Breaking Our DNA

Our brain cells literally break our DNA to make memories. Creating damage that neurons must repair is important to our memory and learning. Over time, some people's brains stop the repairs. When that happens, the brain starts to deteriorate along with the memory and ability to learn new things.

It's weird that what allows us to have memories is the thing that might also take those memories away.

* * *

I sit back so hard, my head smacks the wall. I barely hear what else Yakov says. All I can think of is Gram hiding in a closet from her own father.

I think about her visiting her mother in the hospital and then having to go home to the man who put her there. How did she live with the memories? Was this why she was forgetting?

"This is it," I say, interrupting Yakov mid-sentence. "This must be why she's losing her memory. The trauma is too much for her."

Yakov looks at me with his mouth twisted, like he wants to cry. Doesn't he understand what I'm saying? I want to scream at him, to make him see I've found the answer.

"This is it," I say again. "I can help her now. I can give her back the right memories and take away the painful ones."

"Why is she forgetting sixty years after it happened? If it were the trauma, wouldn't it have happened sooner?" he asks gently. Almost like he's afraid I'm the one about to cry.

I open my mouth and close it. I don't have an answer for this.

"I have a perfect memory," I finally say. "I can remember everything that's ever happened to me. I can remember like it's happened just a second ago."

My scattered thoughts settle in a pattern I recognize. I swallow past the sudden lump in my throat and keep talking. "It doesn't seem fair that I have so many memories but she's losing all of hers."

He rubs his jaw, listening carefully.

"Our brains are very complex," I say. "Scientists change what they believe all the time, and I've been studying how we make memories. How our brain stores them . . ." I don't know what I want to say. What if he's right? That the traumatic thing I've been trying to find isn't the reason Gram's forgetting? What if there's no cure and all of this was for nothing?

"It is true that our brains are complex," Yakov says, each word measured. "But sometimes people get sick. Did you know that Tatyana's mother had Alzheimer's? It happened when she was even younger than Tatyana is now."

"No one told me," I say. Why hadn't Dad said anything about his grandma? Was this why he suspected Alzheimer's in the first place? All my theories are spinning out of control.

"It was a painful thing for your *babushka*. Olga was everything to her growing up. She was very protective of her mother."

"Olga?" That was the name Alexei used. He'd been talking about Gram's mother.

Someone pounds on the door. "You guys done yet?" Max says loudly.

Yakov nods to the door. "Should I let them in?"

I nod, all of my energy gone. I don't know what to do anymore. If I can't fix Gram's memory by helping her remember, then what else is left for me to do?

Olivia rushes in like she expects to find me murdered.

"Find out anything good?" Max's gaze darts between Yakov and me.

"I can't help my gram," I say, trying not to cry.

"You can help her," Yakov says, touching his finger to my temple. "You save all her memories up here. In this magnificent brain. You keep them safe for her, and then you can tell them to her. You say she tells you her stories, *da*?"

I blink away the salt of my tears. I don't even care that I'm crying in front of Max.

"Then you tell them back to her. When she doesn't know them, then you remind her. As long as you remember, she will never be gone."

My tears drip down my cheeks. I wipe them off with the tissue Yakov hands me.

Max puts an arm around my shoulders in a quick side hug. "Can I ask him something?" he whispers to me.

"Go ahead. But I'm ninety-nine percent sure he isn't a spy."

"Hey!" Max shakes his head at me, his eyes wide in mock horror. "Let's hope he isn't because I'm pretty sure we're in major trouble after you just gave us away."

A giggle pushes past my tears, and Max grins at me.

Olivia rolls her eyes and turns to Yakov. "He

wants to ask about the file the government has on her gram. It's, like, all marked out in black or something. We thought it might be because she's a spy."

Yakov's laughter barks out in harsh rumbles. His entire body shakes with it. Even Olivia can't stop a quick laugh of surprise at the force of it.

"Her papa was very influential in the Russian government. He would have been able to track them anywhere they went. Mark made sure he'd never find them and hurt them again. He must have classified whatever information the United States had on Tatyana and Olga. It would be the only way he could have kept them safe, *da*?"

Olivia's mouth forms a perfect circle. Max's grin slips right off his face. "That's messed up," Max mutters.

They walk with me as Yakov leads us to the front yard. Yakov's heavy hand lands on my shoulder. "Little Tatyana, please come visit me, *da*? You and I will be friends, and I will tell you all my stories about your *babushka*. We will keep her memories safe."

"I will," I say. I duck my head and mumble a goodbye, and we trudge to the bus stop in silence. Max and Olivia are both quiet until we're in front of my house.

"The man in the woods who called your gram a traitor," Max says. "Was it Yakov?"

My head snaps up.

"Dude, how could you forget about that?" he asks with a wry grin.

"She's had other things on her mind obviously," Olivia says, turning to me with a sympathetic grimace. "Are you going to ask your gram about what Yakov told you?"

"I don't know." I feel lost. I found the traumatic memory. I solved the mystery of Gram's past. But none of it matters. It didn't fix anything, and I don't know what to do about Gram. How can I make sure my parents don't send her away if I can't help her?

"I think you should," Olivia says. "My mom says all stories are like pancakes. There are always two sides, and you won't know her side if you don't ask."

I stare at my house. I'm not sure I'm ready to be on my own with all this new information. Almost as if they can sense what I'm thinking, Max and Olivia both follow me inside the yard.

"Lulu's gram is the best cook," Olivia says, her shoulder bumping mine.

"I'm pretty hungry," Max says, rubbing his hands together and raising his eyebrows.

I laugh. "You guys want to come in? My mom might be weird, just warning you."

Max shakes his head. "No one is weirder than my mom."

"Um, guys," Olivia says, raising her hand. "I win that contest."

I try to look at my house through Max's eyes. The neat brick walkway, the blue hydrangeas lining the house like a blue ribbon. The black door that Dad painted last month. Clay's toys cluttered around the entry along with neatly lined-up shoes.

"They take their shoes off here," Olivia tells Max.

"Yeah, yeah, I remember," Max says, slipping his

work boots off and doing his best to line them up with the rest of the shoes.

I turn to hide my smile.

"Lulu," Gram calls out when the front door shuts. "We're in the kitchen."

Mom is at the stove. "How was your ride?" She smiles wide when she catches sight of Olivia and Max. "Oh, hello there."

"I invited Max and Olivia for dinner. Is that okay?"

"Of course," Mom says. "Please introduce me to your friend."

"Okay," I say. "Mom, this is Olivia—"

"Ha ha," Mom says with a knowing smile. "Since Olivia is here more than your dad, I think it's safe *she's* not who I'm talking about."

Max holds out a hand. "Hello. I'm Max Rodriguez."

"Nice to meet you, Max. Please have a seat. We're eating in a few minutes, as soon as my husband gets home."

We wash our hands. Olivia flicks water on Max and then me. He starts to retaliate but thinks better of it when he looks over my shoulder. "Your gram keeps staring at me," Max whispers. "Do you think she knows what we've been doing?"

"No," I assure him. I can't tell him that Gram thinks I have a crush on him. There's only so much humiliation I can handle in one day.

The front door slams and Clay drops his toys. "Dada, Dada," he chants when Dad walks in. Mom introduces him to Max, and I want to die when he narrows his eyes at Max and then frowns at me. Is it too much to hope that one person in my family won't embarrass me?

Dinner goes better than I expect. Gram is herself, and she keeps Max in the conversational loop. I stay quiet, trying to make sense of all the new things I know about my family. Things I've always taken for granted look different now.

Mom's swirling finger in the air doesn't mean she wishes she were somewhere else. It means she's chosen to be here. Dad's absentminded smile is still a smile, and it's full of his love for us. Clay is just . . . Clay. Funny, loud, and sometimes a brat, but most of the time sweet. Gram's not a spy or someone I never knew. There's a whole part of her life she's kept to herself, but it's what made her the kind of grandmother who loves every last bit of me, even the parts no one else sees.

I think Mom is trying. Our talk appears to have changed something for the better. She seems almost as happy as she does when she's painting. Dad notices and can't stop smiling his goofy smile. They keep touching hands and calling each other "babe," which is weird, but also sort of sweet.

After Max and Olivia leave, Dad heads to his office to finish some work, Mom takes Clay to bed, and I help Gram do the dishes. Lately the dishwasher's buttons have been confusing her, and it's easier for her to do the dishes by hand. I make sure they are put away in the right cabinet so Dad won't have to hunt for his favorite mug like he did last week. I had found it in the freezer when I grabbed Clay a Popsicle, and I'm not sure how much longer I can keep my parents from noticing things like mugs in the freezer.

Gram hands me the clean dishes and I dry them. The mindless rhythm we develop feels effortlessly efficient, like so many other things with Gram. When the last dish is done, she turns to me.

"Yakov called," she says. "I think we should talk, yes?"

33.

Myelin

Around the axon is a fatty white substance called myelin. Its job is to protect the axon—kind of like a phone charger cable that has plastic around the wires. This protection helps the electrical signal travel way faster. The signal may still get through without the myelin, but it takes longer to get there. People who don't have enough myelin get diseases that make it hard to walk or think clearly.

We all do better with a little protection around us. Without it, we might be so afraid we'll make a wrong choice that we refuse to make any at all.

Gram's eyes are so soft with love, it takes me a moment to grasp her question. "I believe you have something of mine?"

My skin goes hot. I imagine my blood bubbling like when Gram makes soup. I'm a serving of guilt soup ready to be poured out.

I hurry to my backpack and pull out the journal, handing it to her, my cheeks burning bright. "I'm sorry, Gram. I know it was wrong to take it."

She holds it against her chest. "I promised to give it to you one day, didn't I?"

I swallow past the tight grasp of my throat. How does she remember telling me that but not remember how to use the dishwasher?

"Yes."

"Did you take it to help me?" She flips through, stopping to read one section more thoroughly.

"I took it before you started telling me your stories," I try to explain, but it sounds lame even to my own ears. "I wanted to help with your memory. I thought . . . It doesn't matter what I thought."

"You thought if you could find the bad memory I was trying so hard to forget, that it would help me, yes?" She looks up from the journal, the tired droop of her eyelid nearly covering her eye.

"I did."

Gram smiles gently. "I know you worry about me," she says. "I promised Yakov that I would go see a real doctor this time. He is making me an appointment with someone he knows who is a specialist with this kind of thing."

Click. The air shimmers with a memory of Gram taking me to the hospital. I had croup. Each breath was such an effort, it was like breathing through a heavy blanket. Gram kept me calm, made sure I took my medicine, sang me songs until I finally fell asleep in a steam of cold air permeating my lungs. She never left me alone.

"I'll go with you," I say, blinking past my tears. Logically, I know tears are a hormonal response from my endocrine system. Knowing this still doesn't stop them from overflowing.

Gram takes my face in her hands. "Oh, my sweet girl. You *have* been worried. I'm so sorry you've carried this for so long. I think you must have questions for me?"

I sniff and wipe my face with the palm of my hand. "Why didn't you tell me the truth about your dad?"

She drops her hands to her sides and sighs. "It seemed easier to tell you about it if it wasn't about me. I didn't want you to think of me sad or in danger. I didn't want to scare you."

I snort.

Gram nods with a small, worried smile. "Yes, I can see now that all I did was scare you. By keeping things from you, I've made it worse. But I think that for many years I lied to myself, too. To keep safe—to not think about those horrible times—I pretended it had happened to Jacob. Even in my journal I said it was Jacob's papa. I said it so much, I started to believe it."

"You believed your own lie?" I ask, eyes wide.

Gram nods. "If I believed it, then it wasn't a lie, you see?"

I think about this. How we can even lie to ourselves.

"Did Mark help you escape because he loved your mom?"

She looks past me. "I think he must have. My mama didn't think of him that way at first. She was too worn and tired when we first moved here. But I think his kindness finally won her over. She wasn't used to being treated as if she mattered."

I can't imagine what Gram must have seen. I hate to think about it. My dad might work too much, but he'd never hurt Mom, Clay, or me. I always feel safe with him.

Why have I been afraid to tell him about Gram? Or about me and my memory? I'm treating him like he's the enemy, and he's not.

"When Mark and my mama were first married," Gram says, so softly I can barely hear her, "I used to walk in and find them dancing. Sometimes without music. And the way Mark looked at her? It's how she always deserved to be loved. It made all my homesickness seem small and unworthy."

"Did you think of Mark as your dad?" I ask. I can't imagine having any dad other than my own. I don't want to.

"Eventually, yes," Gram says, stifling a yawn. "It's getting late, though. One more question and then bed for you, sweet girl."

I have too many questions firing through my neurons. I bite my lip as I think about which one to ask. I remember Max's earlier question.

"Do you remember a time when I was a little girl and we were in Samuel P. Taylor Park and a man yelled at you in Russian? Was it Yakov?"

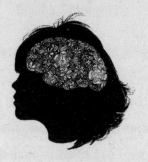

34.
Nodes of Ranvier

The nodes of Ranvier are the gaps between the myelin on an axon. You would think a gap would slow the nerve signal down, but the signal leaps along each gap and supercharges for the next leap. This makes transmission faster. It's like using a ramp to make a jump on your bike.

Sometimes we have to jump over things in our way—hurdles that may seem like they're slowing us down, but they actually get us there faster.

I'm curled up in a ball on my bed when Olivia FaceTimes me later that night.

She sighs dramatically. "I've been thinking—"

"The Russian man I saw at Samuel P. Taylor Park was Yakov," I interrupt in a rush. "He was telling Gram she couldn't run from love forever. That she was betraying them if she did."

She leans closer to the phone, her eyes huge. "Your gram told you?"

"Yeah, we talked. She wants to answer all my questions." My pillow is wet with tears. Just when I think I can't cry any more, they start all over again. I know the truth about everything, but none of it matters. I can't fix anything.

"I'm so sorry, Lulu. Did she tell you why she hid her passports?"

"Yeah. I guess Mark smuggled them out through France. It was their backstory here if anyone asked where they were from. Because of that, Gram and her mom were legally French citizens. Gram hid the passports because she'd never told my dad the whole truth and she didn't want him to stumble across them."

"Wow! You could totally write a book about this one day," Olivia says with a shake of her head.

"I just want to sleep. Maybe when I wake up, this will all have been a bad dream."

Olivia nods, and her mouth pulls down. "I know exactly how that feels."

"I know you do," I say, wiping my eyes. "You're going through so much, and this whole day has been about me. I'm the one who should say 'I'm sorry' to you."

"Nope, don't even go there. You're my best friend. I love you. You're there for me, and I'm there for you."

"I love you too. I don't know how I would have gotten through today without you and Max." I prop my phone against my pillow and smile as she rolls her eyes.

"Yeah, Max is okay, I guess," she says. "He was really worried about you."

My heart does the dance of a hundred butterflies. "That's nice of him."

She snorts. "Yeah, right, it's because he's so *nice*. Whatever you need to tell yourself. Okay, then, I'll text you tomorrow."

"Tomorrow, yep."

I hang up and cradle my phone. With Olivia gone, sadness mixes with a smattering of hope in my neurotransmitters.

The room dims and I close my eyes. I drift off slowly when something triggers my hypothalamus. It fires up and kicks me with a healthy dose of adrenaline.

I sit up in bed with a gasp, my chest heaving like I've run out of air. Silence fills the night with darkness and shadows. What woke me? I grab my phone. The glowing clock shows me it's too early to be up. I slip out of bed. The hallway is quiet, but the rumblings of Dad's snores filter through the walls.

I head down to the kitchen for a snack, pausing at Gram's room. Her door is wide open.

"Gram?" I keep my voice low in case she's sleeping. She always shuts her door. I can't recall a time when she's left it open at night.

I walk closer, listening for the light whistle of her snores. The quiet is eerie. Every part of me strains to hear a sound. But all I hear are the quick gasps of my own breathing.

"Gram," I say again, louder this time.

I push open her door. The crumpled mess of her covers shows in the dim light of her bedside clock. Her bed is empty. The room is empty. The bathroom is dark and empty.

My heart clunks painfully against my ribs. Where is she? I'd read that people with Alzheimer's might be more disoriented at night than during the day, and I flash back to the night I found her crying in her room. It even has a name: sundowning. They aren't sure why it happens, but it might have something to do with emotional or physical stimulation during the day.

Today had been filled with a buttload of emotional and physical stimulation.

I check the kitchen and am on my way to the living room when I notice the front door wide open. Fog dampens the air and blows a cold breeze into the house.

I grab my coat out of the closet and shove my

feet into my boots. All the cars are parked in the driveway, and I let out the breath I was holding. At least she isn't driving around in the middle of the night. A gust of air slams the door behind me.

The air chills my bones. The fog is thick against the dull light of the streetlamps. I call for her, softly at first, but louder as I make my way down the road.

"Lulu!" Dad's voice comes from the direction of the house. The weak gleam of a flashlight shines in my direction.

"Dad?" My voice breaks. Water drips down my nose and cheeks. I'm not sure if it's fog or tears.

"What are you doing outside?" he asks, each word clipped like when he's trying not to yell.

My silence stretches out despite any effort I make to talk. Nothing comes out of my mouth but gulping sobs.

He stops a foot away, the flashlight on my face like he's making sure it's really me.

"I . . . I'm looking for Gr-Gram," I explain.

"Why are you looking for Gram? Is she gone?"

His voice is rough and stark, stripped bare of his usual confidence.

I wave my arm around, trying to find the right direction. "She's not in her room. I think she's out here somewhere."

He steps closer, aiming the flashlight past the bushes and driveways lining the streets. He holds his arms out for me, and I fly into them. He squeezes me so tight I can barely breathe.

I pull away. Every second is important right now.

"I woke up and Gram was gone. I think she's been gone for a while."

He stares down at me, trying to process what I've said. "Why would she go outside in the cold and dark?"

"We, um, had a really big talk about her past," I say. "I think that might make her more forgetful or something."

"Forgetful?" he says with a quick shake of his head. "As in she doesn't remember things? But the doctor cleared her. He said it was a vitamin deficiency."

"She never really went to the doctor. It was a

friend who pretended to be one." I hang my head and stare at the dark shadows playing across the street. Guilt slices through my bones and guts me. "I've done research, and if it is Alzheimer's, then she's still in the early stages. Each case is different, though, so she may have episodes like this, but it doesn't mean she needs to be in a home. She can still function."

Everything I've been afraid of is happening. Will he send Gram away for this?

"Lulu, sweetie, Gram doesn't have Alzheimer's. I think I would notice if her memory was that bad."

"Not if I covered for her." I say the words like they are slivers of glass in my mouth.

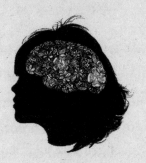

35.

Saltatory Conduction

The word "saltatory" means to jump. The nerve gets the signal, the signal hops from node to node, and the signal arrives at its destination.

Saltatory conduction helps nerve impulses travel faster and take up less space. This helps us think and act faster. Right now I need to think and act fast—I need to make Dad understand how important Gram is to our family.

Dad stares at me as if I'm someone he doesn't know. "What do you mean you covered for her?"

"I was afraid of losing her," I explain. "I didn't want her to go to a retirement home, so I didn't tell you when she got lost or couldn't remember something. I was trying to find a way to fix her. I thought if I could find out about her past, I could help her."

He shakes his head. "Who said anything about a retirement home?"

"I found the brochure in your office."

He looks at me, his brow furrowed. "Gram gave me that. She said she wanted her own space."

The flashlight shines on the sidewalk. I think about how the cracks fanning out in the concrete are what my heart feels like. "When did she say that?" I ask slowly.

"About a month ago. I noticed she didn't seem herself, so I suggested she see a doctor. She came to me with the brochure and said this might be something we should look at, and I told her not to be ridiculous. When she said she went to the doctor, I believed her. She just said he told her to rest a little more."

He starts walking, sweeping the flashlight back and forth as he searches. "Mom," he calls out. "Where are you?"

I hurry to catch up to him. There's movement down on the street corner. I point. "Over there."

Dad trains the flashlight to where I've pointed. He exhales in relief. "There she is."

I run to her. She turns to me, her mouth rounded in fear. "Lulu, what are you doing out in this cold?"

"We were looking for you." I throw my arms around her. Her skin is icy to the touch. "You're so cold, Gram."

"Nonsense," she says, patting my arms. "I'm from Moscow. We thrive in this weather."

Dad walks up behind me. "Ma, what are you doing out here? It's freezing. Let's get you home."

"I was taking a walk. No need for all the fuss."

Dad shrugs out of his jacket and wraps it around her. I notice for the first time that she's wearing only a thin nightgown. "You had us worried, Mom."

She touches a hand to his cheek. "How sweet of you."

"Why were you out this time of night?" he asks gently.

Gram doesn't answer. She seems to shrink inside herself as we walk home.

Once we're home, Dad turns to me. "Why don't you help Gram to bed, and I'll make us a snack so we can talk."

I nod, tightening my grip on Gram's hand so she doesn't slip away.

"Lulu," he bites out, then stops. He takes a deep breath and continues in a calmer voice. "I'm sorry you felt you couldn't come to me."

I make myself look at him. He gives me a half smile before bending down to kiss Gram's cheek.

Gram pats his face. "You need a shave."

He laughs and ruffles my hair before I lead Gram to her room and settle her in bed. "Gram, you can't leave the house at night. It isn't safe."

She squeezes my hand a second before letting go. "I think I owe you a story, Lulu. Have I told you about my friend Jacob? He loved to play chess with me. But I always beat him."

My smile freezes like the Russian lake in Gram's story. I pull the covers up over her shoulders and fold them neatly. "Tell me tomorrow, Gram. Right now you need to sleep."

Click. All the memories of Gram tucking me in. Each kiss forever accessible in the movie of my life. I take one out and let it play as I tuck her in now. I kiss her forehead as she always did with me. I mirror her actions back to her, and my heart cracks all over again.

"Good night, Gram," I say softly before I close the door.

"Good night, my sweet girl," she whispers.

The worry of what to do no longer seems like a problem I'll never solve. Mom and Dad are in the kitchen. Their voices reach me, low but warm as they wait for me to join them.

It's not always easy to know what the right thing to do is. When you love someone, you try to protect them. Like Mom and Dad did with each other, like Yakov and I did with Gram. Like Gram did for Clay and me.

My parents have made mistakes. But so have I.

Mom turns to me when I walk into the kitchen. She brushes the hair out of my face and leans her forehead against mine. "Your dad told me. I'm so sorry you thought you had to figure this out on your own."

Dad comes over, and we make it a group hug. Their embrace is safety and love. It's the way I used to feel with them. It's the way I can feel again. The electricity humming in my brain quiets, and the picture of this moment clicks into place. If I trust them with Gram, then I know I can trust them with me, too.

I take a breath. "I need to tell you something about my memory."

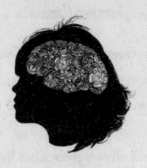

36.
Von Economo Neurons

Our insula would be nothing without von Economo neurons, or VENs. These are slug-shaped cells found mostly in the insula. Without these cells, we would never turn our feelings into actions.

When we crave something like pancakes, it's because we remember the smell and taste, but it's also because we remember how we felt when we ate them. Like when Gram made me a Minnie Mouse–shaped pancake, the kitchen was warm and Clay was laughing while I made faces at him. Emotional moments affect how we remember. I'm happy when I smell pancakes because it reminds me of Gram making them for me.

I know I will always remember how I feel at this second here with Gram. We're alone in the house since my parents took Clay to the park. I sip my hot chocolate and nibble at the cinnamon roll she's made. The entire house smells like warm sugar and vanilla.

"I'm thrilled you told your parents about your memory," she says.

"They were pretty amazing about it, actually." I shrug, trying to act like it's no big deal. My mouth doesn't cooperate, and I can't hold back a smile.

"Well, I won't say I told you so. . . ." Gram's eyes sparkle.

I laugh. "But you told me so."

She holds her hand up in an exaggerated shrug. Her smile fades after a second and her expression turns serious. "I'm sorry for scaring you last night."

"I think it was because you were emotional about . . ." I point to the journal.

"Perhaps," she acknowledges. "Yakov called me again this morning to check up on me. He wanted me to tell you to come see him again."

"You and Yakov," I say, picking my way slowly through what I want to ask. "Why can't . . . ? Why can't you be together now? He still loves you. You know that, right?"

"And I will always love him." She picks up the journal. "I want to read you my last entry. I've told you most of it, but this will finish the story, yes?"

I scoot closer and she begins to read. She translates as she reads and remembers. Her accent thickens, the words slow and heavy:

> *Tatyana's journal:*
> *June 7, 1968*
> My beloved journal, you have traveled with me through many a hard time, and I will always be grateful to Mama for insisting I write in you. I write this last entry on my wedding day. No more writing in Russian after this.

I am marrying a wonderful man who loves me dearly. I thought I would never love again, or at least not as much as I love Jacob (for I still love him—I always will). But then I met Daniel. He is smart, funny, and passionate about so many of the same things I am. I know we will have a wonderful life together.

He knows about Russia and Papa. He knows everything, and I trust him to keep my secrets. I never see Jacob and Margaret, but we still keep in touch. To cut the thread would be to kill us. I need to know he is safe, and he needs to know I am happy.

They have a son, a little boy named Bobby. I hope to have children one day soon. I hope it will be a little girl who I can someday tell my stories to. I will tell her about Russia when she is old enough to understand. Perhaps we will travel there one day together.

Daniel asks if I wish to visit Papa. I think I won't dare it. It would destroy Mama if she knew. I do miss him, despite how he treated us. He will always be my papa. But it is best to forget, I think. So, for now, I will shut that part of my life away. I will close this book and begin another. Finally.

I dream of love, of happiness, of a life well lived. I believe my Daniel and I will have all these things.

Gram's voice trembles with emotion as she speaks about my grandfather. Her love flows from her journal and out into the air around her. I file it away. Each second, each minute.

Gram closes the book and rests her hand on the top. "And we did. We had a good life full of love, and I don't regret any of it. Jacob is married, and I cannot ever get in the way of a marriage. We are what we were in the beginning—the very best of friends. It is enough."

"But . . . don't you want to be together?" I think about how feelings can change over time, and I can't help but think of how I used to feel about

Max. How the smirk I used to find so irritating is now sort of cute.

"We are together," she says patiently. "We are best friends, and we always will be. It is true and strong, and sometimes this is better than the romance."

I'm not sure I like this explanation. It isn't the happy ending I want. But maybe there are different kinds of happy endings. Not everything happens the way we want it to. All the areas of our brains— neurotransmitters, glial cells, neurons, and the many things I've studied to make sense of how memory works—are interconnected and work in a spectacular way.

Until they don't.

"Did Yakov tell you what I told him about your memory loss?" I ask gently.

She grimaces and nods abruptly. "Yes. I hope it isn't true. Do I really forget so much? I know I get confused at times. And, of course, last night was concerning. But surely it's not too bad?"

I promised my parents I would tell Gram the truth, so I do. "You forget something every day," I say, spitting my words out fast so I can't take them back. "Sometimes, for just a second, you even forget who I am."

She closes her eyes briefly, but not before I see the flicker of pain. "You need to promise me something, Lulu."

"Yes, Gram?"

She looks straight at me, her gaze piercing the exposed fragments of my heart. "You will put all this away in your phenomenal memory and keep it safe. Can you do that for me?"

I nod, giant tears plopping onto my knees. "I will."

"If I'm like my mama, then it will take years for me to completely forget. In the meantime, keep reminding me, yes? And I will try to listen. You will make me listen. You will tell me my stories. The ones I give to you."

"Every day," I promise.

"It's how I keep my mama alive," she says with a sad smile. "I remember her life. As long as you have those little pieces of them, then the person is never really gone. They're always close by."

She seems to know, as she always does, what I need. She opens her arms to me, and I hug her tight, absorbing the deceptive strength of her as she gathers me close on her lap.

"Gram," I say, "how do you say 'I love you' in Russian?"

Her fingers thread gently through my hair. "*Ya tebya lyublyu.*"

I repeat the words slowly, imagining Gram's mother saying them to her. "*Lyublyu,*" I whisper.

We stay this way until her arms tremble with my weight, until I have no more tears left, until she's answered every last one of my questions.

37.
Lulu's Journal

July 20, 2019

    Gram gave me this journal to help me make sense of everything happening. She says if I write down what I'm afraid of, it won't have such power over me.

    My name is Lulu Rose Carter, and I'm twelve, almost thirteen. I love reading books and riding my horse, Remy, and I love my family.

If this summer taught me anything, it's that just because you forget something doesn't mean it didn't happen. It's still written in the pathways of your heart and the hearts of those you love. Our memories are fragile. They break easily and with no real reason. But the emotions they carve in our souls last forever.

Gram's hand in mine, her pancakes on cold mornings, her no-nonsense laugh, the way she listens to me, the love in her eyes when she watches Clay play, the patience when Mom needed it, the strength when she helped Dad keep his family together. Gram is in each of these memories.

I will never forget.

I fill a notebook with Gram's stories. But I also begin to write my own. And I'm starting to understand why Mom paints, and how art can help make sense of life.

The Memory Keeper

A story for Clay: "The Brave Knight"
There was once a girl who swallowed her grandmother's memory. It grew inside her and gave her the ability to remember everything. A special power that brought with it great responsibility.

The girl tried to give her grandmother back the memory. But she learned that memories are mysterious and deeply personal. How we see them depends on who we are.

The girl traveled the world looking for a cure for her grandmother. Her faithful friends helped her find a man from a distant land who promised to have all the answers. Only, his answers created more questions, until everything she knew was a tangled maze.

Then, one day, she found a book of memories. The girl read the book to her grandmother every day. Every night her grandmother would visit the girl in her dreams, and this was the only place the girl felt truly loved.

Loneliness plagued the girl until she finally confessed to her parents all she'd done. Her father and mother opened their hearts to the girl. They promised to care for her grandmother, but there was nothing they could do to make her well again. And this was when the girl learned that some things have no cure.

The girl's extraordinary memory was the only solution. She would keep a file in her brain. Each memory labeled and stored safely forever.

This is how the girl became the Memory Keeper. She filed her grandmother's memories with a secret key. Only the bravest knight with the noblest heart could access the memories. The key, my noble knight, is a top secret riddle. Solve it and the treasure is yours.

The Memory Keeper

What fills the cracks in a heart
And is stronger than glue?
In the Russian language
It rhymes with "you."

Lyublyu
люблю

Acknowledgments

Thank you to the many people who have made this book possible:

Stacey Glick, my fabulous agent, thank you for believing in me and helping me believe in myself.

Tricia Lin, my whip-smart editor, a million thanks for understanding Lulu and helping me uncover her story. For patiently answering all my questions. And, most of all, thank you for making this whole experience a joyful one.

A huge thank-you to the entire team at Aladdin: Alyson Heller, Mara Anastas, Heather Palisi, Mike Rosamilia, Katherine Devendorf, Sara Berko, Caitlin Sweeny, Michelle Leo, and Nicole Russo. Thank you, Aveline Stokart, for my spectacular cover. I couldn't love it more! Thanks to my copy editor, Penina Lopez, for your detailed edits and for catching my inconsistencies. Thank you, also, to Amy Cloud for being the first one to fall in love with *The Memory Keeper* and for bringing me to the Aladdin/S&S family.

Acknowledgments

I want to thank all my first readers: Nicole Hohmann, Kimberly Gabriel, Kimberly MacCarron, Annette Christy, Gia Camiccia, Christine Grissom, Taylor Gardner, Liz Edelbrock, and Elise Bungo. Shout-out to my literati critique group: Suzi Guina, Kaitlin Hundscheid, Tara Creel, Katie Nelson, and Heidi Lang. A special thanks to Malia and Renée for helping me with the Russian words and names in the book.

Thanks to my Pitch Wars mentor, Kristin Wright, for showing me how to revise, and to Brenda Drake for starting such a great contest. Thanks to all my Pitch Wars 2016 people who let me vent and always encourage me to continue writing. Thank you to my Golden Heart sisters, the Rebelles, who inspire me with how hard they work and how supportive they continue to be. And thanks to all the talented writers in my Novel Nineteens debut group and the Class of 2K19 books.

If we are mindful of the small moments that make our lives special, then each of us can be memory keepers for those we love, and they in turn for us.

Acknowledgments

For my family:

Thank you, Stanley, for always supporting me and never complaining when we have pizza for dinner. Thank you to Nicolas, for telling everyone I was a writer way before I thought of myself as one. To Tessa Jewel, who is always my first reader. Thank you for your honesty and belief in me—you always make each book better. To Vince, who told me to remember Dr. Seuss, and to never give up on my dream. I hope I've inspired you to reach for yours. And thank you to Lucas, for offering to be my agent while I was querying and my publisher while I was on sub. You have all given me an abundance of memories to cherish each and every day. I love you more than you'll ever know.

Thank you to Larry McKnight, who encouraged my love of reading, and to Terry Semerad, who reads everything I write—even when it's a blazing trash fire. To Jean and Stan Camiccia, for watching my children so I can write. I love you all so much!

Thank you to Ryan, Melissa, and John. You made growing up an adventure that I plan to use in many future stories. To Chris—the best dad in the world (next to my husband and my brother, of course). Much appreciation and love to my sisters-in-law, Michele and Allyson. So much love to Stanzi, Jack, Rocco, Prezli, Pixxie, Reilly, and Dylan. Each of you inspires me with your unique personalities. Thank you, Cindy, for your kindness and generosity. To Dominic, thank you for making my daughter happy. Leah, thank you for being a kindred spirit.

To the rest of my extended family in Hawaii. To Aunt Jan who tapped my head and said, "What goes on in there?" after reading one of my books. To Uncle Larry, who always has the best nicknames. To Josh, Tina, and their families—I love you guys.

Finally, a special thank-you to my readers. I hope you enjoyed Lulu's story!

About the Author

Jennifer Camiccia has lived in the wilds of Los Angeles, where she wrote her first book at the tender age of five; Iran, where she developed a fear of camels and a fondness for pistachios; Hawaii, with its balmy breezes and memories of learning to swim; and the San Francisco Bay Area, where she now lives with her children and husband. Visit her online at jencamiccia.com or on Twitter @jencamiccia.

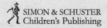 

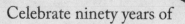

Celebrate ninety years of

NANCY DREW

with this specially redesigned collection
of the first ten Nancy Drew Diaries!